PL

LOVE AND

ENCHANTMENT

THOMAS MANN (1875–1955) was perhaps Germany's most famous twentieth-century writer. Born to a merchant family in Lübeck, Mann was preparing to enter the family business when his father suddenly died and the business was liquidated. The Manns moved to Munich, where Mann began his literary career with the epic novel *Buddenbrooks* (1901), which was a huge success. Further novels and stories followed, including *Death in Venice* (1912) and *The Magic Mountain* (1924); five years following publication of the latter novel, Mann was awarded the Nobel Prize in Literature. When Hitler came to power, Mann fled to Switzerland, and from there he escaped to California at the outbreak of the Second World War. He is buried in Switzerland, where he spent his final years.

LESLEY CHAMBERLAIN is a British writer and critic who has written extensively on German and Russian literature and published three novels.

LOVE AND ENCHANTMENT

THREE STORIES

THOMAS MANN

TRANSLATED FROM THE GERMAN
BY LESLEY CHAMBERLAIN

PUSHKIN PRESS CLASSICS

Pushkin Press
Somerset House, Strand
London WC2R 1LA

English translation and Afterword © 2026 Lesley Chamberlain

Tonio Kröger was first published as *Tonio Kröger* by S. Fischer Verlag in Berlin, 1903

Disorder and Early Sorrow was first published as *Unordnung und frühes Leid* by *Neue Rundschau* in Berlin, 1925

Mario and the Magician was first published as *Mario und der Zauberer* by Velhagens & Klasings Monatshefte, 1930

First published by Pushkin Press in 2026

ISBN 13: 978-1-80533-270-1

A CIP catalogue record for this title is available from the British Library

The authorised representative in the EEA is eucomply OÜ, Pärnu mnt. 139b-14, 11317, Tallinn, Estonia, hello@eucompliancepartner.com, +33757690241

Designed and typeset by Tetragon, London
Printed and bound in the United Kingdom by Clays Ltd, Elcograf S.p.A.

Pushkin Press is committed to a sustainable future for our business, our readers and our planet. This book is made from paper from forests that support responsible forestry.

MIX
Paper | Supporting
responsible forestry
FSC® C018072

www.pushkinpress.com
1 3 5 7 9 8 6 4 2

Contents

TONIO KRÖGER

I

THE SUN THAT WINTER DAY stood above the narrow town as no more than a pale reflection of itself, dull and milky behind the layers of clouds. In the gabled streets it was wet and wind blew round the corners, and now and again something like soft hailstones fell, neither ice nor snow.

School was over for the day. Hordes of youngsters released from its precinct streamed across the cobbled courtyard and out through the latticed gate and went their separate ways, rushing off to right and left. The older boys had a dignified way of holding their packs of books high against their left shoulder, while with their right arms they steered their way against the wind towards lunch; the little ones set off merrily at such a trot that the icy mish-mash sprayed everywhere and *The Essentials of Knowledge* clattered in their sealskin satchels. But then it happened that all of them tore off their caps and respectfully lowered their eyes at the sight of a senior master, with his hat and his beard like a cross between Wotan and Jupiter, coming their way...

'Are you coming, Hans? You're taking ages.' Tonio Kröger had been waiting a long time on the embankment; he smiled as he walked over to his friend, who was coming out of the gate, chatting with other schoolmates and about to go off with them...'What do you mean?' he asked, and looked at Tonio... 'Ah yes, that's right! Just a bit further.'

Tonio fell silent, and his eyes lost their shine. Had Hans forgotten, was he just remembering again now that they had intended to go for a walk this afternoon? Since they agreed it, he himself had been looking forward to the moment, to the exclusion of all else.

'See you then,' said Hans Hansen to his other companions. 'I'll walk on a bit with Kröger.' And the two turned left as the others veered right.

Hans and Tonio had time to go for a walk after school, because both belonged to households that only took their midday meal at four o'clock. Their fathers were important businessmen who held public positions and had a great deal of power in the town. To the Hansens had belonged for generations the extensive timber yards down by the river, where huge mechanical saws carved up the tree trunks with a great deal of whooshing and hissing. But then Tonio was the son of Consul Kröger, and you could see sacks of grain bearing the broad black family imprint being delivered along the streets every day; and the big old house of his ancestors was the most imposing in the whole town...The two friends were forever having to take off their caps because of their wide circles of acquaintance, and many people were first to greet the fourteen-year-olds...

Both had hung their schoolbags over their shoulders, and both were warmly and suitably dressed: Hans in a mariner's short reefer jacket, with the broad blue collar of his sailor suit standing out over the shoulders and back, and Tonio in a grey belted overcoat. Hans wore a Danish sailor's cap with short ribbons, and a chunk of his pale blond hair spilt out from beneath it. He was extremely pretty and finely made, broad in the shoulders and narrow in the hips, with prominent steel-blue eyes that took a sharp view of the world. But beneath Tonio's round fur cap the eyes that looked out from his angular southern face, with its swarthier complexion, were dark and delicately shaded. The eyelids were heavy, and Tonio's glance was dreamy and a bit shy... His mouth and chin were unusually soft and smooth. He walked along casually and unevenly, whereas Hans, with his slender legs in black stockings, marched elastically and keeping perfect time...

Tonio didn't speak. He felt downright hurt. Pulling his rather slanting brows together, and rounding his lips as if to whistle, he stared with his head to one side into the distance. This look and gesture were characteristic of him.

All of a sudden Hans thrust his arm under Tonio's and as he did so cast him a sideways glance, for he understood very well what the matter was. And, while Tonio stayed silent for the next few steps, he fell into a mood that made him seem very vulnerable.

'Actually I didn't forget, Tonio,' said Hans, and looked out ahead on to the pavement, 'I just thought it was probably not going to come to much today, because it's so wet and windy. But I don't mind that at all and I find it terrific that you waited for me anyway. I was already thinking you'd gone home and it made me cross...'

Everything inside Tonio began to dance and sing when he heard those words.

'Right, so we'll walk along the ramparts,' he said with emotion in his voice. 'By way of the Mühlenwall and the Holstenwall, and that way I'll see you home, Hans... I can make my own way back to mine, that's no trouble; and next time you can accompany me.'

In fact he had no great faith in what Hans had said, and felt distinctly that the latter set only half as much store by their walks together as he did. But still he could see that Hans regretted having forgotten, and had taken it upon himself to make things better. And he was very far from rejecting this overture...

For the truth was that Tonio loved Hans Hansen and had already suffered a great deal because of him. The person most deeply in love is always the one who suffers more—is the one at a disadvantage—his fourteen-year-old soul had already taken in this hard and simple lesson; and he was made in such a way that he took good note of such experiences, it was as if he stored them up inside himself, and in a way it gave him pleasure, without its determining any personal course of action or delivering any practical results. It was also to do with the way he was made that such realizations were much more important and interesting to him than any lessons he had to learn at school. Indeed, much of the time spent in lessons under the Gothic vaults of the classroom he devoted to intensifying such emotions as far as they would go. He wanted really to come to grips with them. And this activity gave him the same sort of satisfaction as when he walked about his room playing the violin (for he played the violin) and, producing the notes as quietly as he could, let them mingle with the splashing of the fountain in the garden below, whose rhythmic sound reached up to him from beneath the branches of an old walnut tree...

The fountain, the old walnut tree, his violin and in the distance the sea, the Baltic sea, whose summer dreams he had the privilege of listening in on during the holidays; these were the things that he loved, the things he surrounded himself with, as it were, and in whose midst his inner life happened. The resonant names of those things could be used to good effect in poetry and frequently did find their way into poems Tonio Kröger set down.

That he possessed a book of poems he'd written himself had become known through his own fault and cost him dearly, among his schoolmates and also with the masters. For his part it struck the son of Consul Kröger that it would be stupid and common to take offence, and he despised the other boys, and the teachers too. Their bad manners offended him all the more. Through them he acquired an unusually penetrating insight into their personal weaknesses. On the other hand, he himself judged it indecent and actually inappropriate to write poetry, and he had more or less to concede that all those who took exception and found it an alien activity were right. Only that didn't make it possible for him to stop…

Since he made poor use of his time at home, and was slow and distracted in class, and the masters had a poor opinion of him, he kept bringing home the most pitiful reports. They made his father, a tall, immaculately dressed gentleman with thoughtful blue eyes, who always wore a poppy in his buttonhole, very angry and worried. For Tonio's mother, however, for his beautiful black-haired mother, whose name was Consuelo and who was so completely different from the other women in the town, because once upon a time his father had discovered her on his globetrotting down south and brought her back up here—for Consuelo what marks he got at school was fundamentally unimportant…

Tonio loved his dark and fiery mother, who played the piano and the mandolin, and it made him happy that she didn't torment herself over his dubious position among his fellow human beings. On the other hand, he took the view that his father's anger was more respectable and had more dignity to it, and although his father told him off, he was actually fully in agreement with him, while he found his mother's cheerful indifference a bit out of order. Sometimes his thoughts ran roughly this way: it's enough in itself that I am the way I am, absent-minded, self-willed and concerned with things that bother no one else, and I can't and don't want to change. Yet at the very least it's appropriate that I get into serious trouble because of it. It's perfectly in order that they punish me and don't just pass over it with kisses and music. I mean we're not gypsies in a green caravan, we're respectable people, we belong to Consul Kröger, we're the Kröger family… Not just now and then, actually quite often, he also thought: why am I so peculiar and in conflict with everything, a disappointment to my teachers and strange among the other boys? I mean look at them, the boys who are good scholars and those who are solidly average. They don't find the masters ridiculous, they don't write poetry and they only think things that other people already think and which they can freely express out loud. How correct and in perfect agreement with everyone and everything they must feel! It must be good… So what is it about me, and what will become of me?

This way of reflecting upon himself and his relationship to life played an important role in Tonio's love for Hans Hansen. He loved him in the first place because he was beautiful; but in the second place he loved him because in every facet of life he seemed to be his opposite and counterweight. Hans Hansen was an excellent scholar and also a good chap, who could ride, do gymnastics and swim heroically; he rejoiced in all-round popularity. The masters were almost fond of him, and called him by his first name and helped him in all sorts of ways; the boys were keen that he should think well of them, and in the street both men and women stopped him, grabbed hold of a lock of his pale blond hair sticking out from beneath the Danish seaman's cap and said: 'Good morning, Hans Hansen, with that pretty hair of yours! Are you still top of the class? Say hello to your mother and father, my fine young man…'

That was how Hans Hansen was, and for as long as Tonio had known him he had only to see him to be filled with longing, longing mixed with an envy he could feel burning in his breast, where it had buried itself deeply. What's it like to have such blue eyes, he thought, and to be so at ease with the world, happy, surrounded by companionship, what's it like to be someone like you! Everything you do, always, is just what respectable people expect and admire. No sooner have you finished your homework than you have a riding lesson, or you work on something with a fretsaw, and even in the holidays, at the seaside, you're always busy rowing and sailing and swimming, whereas I just lie in the sand doing nothing much, a bit lost, and stare out at the mysteriously changing patterns rushing across the face of the water. That's why your eyes are so clear. How it would be to be like you! Just think!

He didn't try to become like Hans Hansen, and perhaps he didn't even seriously wish it. But he desired so painfully to be loved by him. To be loved as he was. And he had his way of seeking that love. It was a slow, sincere way, wistful and full of devotion and melancholy; on the other hand it was melancholy that burned more deeply and all-consumingly in him than ever fierce passion did, despite what might have been expected from his foreign appearance.

The campaign was not entirely in vain, for it must be said that Hans recognized a certain superiority in Tonio, a certain verbal dexterity which allowed him to express difficult things, and he had no difficulty grasping that an unusually strong and tender feeling for him was at work here. He showed his gratitude and frequently made Tonio happy with his reciprocal gestures—but just as often too he left him feeling jealous, disappointed and despairing that he could ever create a spiritual oneness between them. For the peculiar thing was that Tonio, for all that he envied Hans Hansen his way of being, constantly strove to draw him over into his own ways, which could only ever happen in an odd moment; and even then perhaps he was deceiving himself...

'I read something fantastic, really superb...' he said. They were walking along together sharing a bag of fruit sweets they'd bought for ten pfennigs at Iversen's the grocer's in the Mühlenstraße. 'You have to read it, Hans, it's Schiller's *Don Carlos*... I'll lend it to you if you want.'

'Oh no,' said Hans Hansen. 'Leave it, Tonio, that's not for me. I'll stick with my horse books, you know? I tell you the pictures in them are the tops. I'll show you when you next come round. They are photographs taken in slow motion, and you can see the stallions trotting and cantering and jumping, in all the paces that you can't normally see because the movement is too fast.'

'In all paces?' asked Tonio politely. 'Yes, that's super. Only the thing about *Don Carlos* is it's immeasurable. There are moments in it, you'll see, that are so beautiful that they give you a jolt, it's somehow explosive…'

'Explosive?' asked Hans Hansen… 'How do you mean?'

'Well, for example the place where the King weeps because the Marquis has betrayed him… but the Marquis has only betrayed him for the sake of the Prince, for whom he's sacrificing himself. Don't you see? And now comes the news out of the chamber, into the court, that the King had been weeping. "He wept? The King wept?" All the courtiers are dumbstruck, it shatters them, for the King is a terrifyingly severe, merciless figure. But it really sinks in that he wept, and actually I myself am more sorry for him than for the Prince and the Marquis together. He is always so alone and without love, and now he thought he had found someone, and that someone betrayed him…'

Hans Hansen looked at Tonio's face from the side, and something in it won him over to what Tonio was saying, for he suddenly put his arm under Tonio's and asked him:

'In what way did he betray him, Tonio?'

Tonio became excited.

'The point is,' he began, 'that all the letters to Brabant and Flanders…'

'Ah look there's Erwin Jimmerthal coming our way,' said Hans.

Tonio fell silent. And may the Earth swallow up this Jimmerthal, he thought, damn him! Why should he come and disturb us? What if he walks with us the whole way and talks about his riding lessons... For, yes, Erwin Jimmerthal was also learning to ride. He was the son of the bank manager and lived out this way beside the Gate. He came along the alleyway towards them with his bandy legs and narrow eyes, already without his satchel.

'Good day to you, Jimmerthal. I'm just out for a walk with Kröger...'

'I have to go into town,' said Jimmerthal, 'and fetch something. But I can join you part of the way. I say, are those fruit sweets you've got there, thanks, I'll take a couple. We've got another lesson tomorrow, Hans.' He meant a riding lesson.

'Topping!' said Hans. 'I'm getting some leather chaps, don't you know, because I came first in the test we just did...'

'Are you not learning to ride, Kröger?' asked Jimmerthal, and his eyes were just a pair of empty slits.

'No...' answered Tonio, in a markedly uncertain tone.

'You should ask your father to get you some riding lessons too, Kröger,' observed Hans Hansen.

'Yes...' said Tonio hastily, not caring one way or another. But for a moment he couldn't swallow, his throat closed up, because Hans had used his surname; Hans seemed to sense it, for he said by way of an explanation:

'I call you Kröger because your first name is so daft, forgive me, dear friend, but I can't stand it. Tonio... that's not a name at all. On the other hand, you can't do anything about it, that's hard luck.'

'No, the reason that's the case is because your name sounds so foreign and out of the ordinary...' said Jimmerthal, and made it seem as if his had to be the last word.

Tonio's mouth twitched. He pulled himself together and said:

'Yes, it's a stupid name. God knows I'd much rather be called Heinrich or Wilhelm, believe me. But it comes from the fact that a brother of my mother's is called Antonio, and I was baptized after him; you see, my mother comes from a different country...'

Then he went quiet and left the other two to talk about horses and leather chaps. Hans had grabbed hold of Jimmerthal and was talking with an energy and appreciation that *Don Carlos* would never have awakened in him... From time to time Tonio felt he was going to cry, there was a prickle in his nose; he was also struggling to stop his jaw from trembling...

Hans couldn't stand Tonio's name—what was to be done about that? His name was Hans, and Jimmerthal's name was Erwin, fair enough, those were both generally recognized forenames that didn't alienate anyone. But Tonio was exotic and something out of the ordinary. In fact there was something out of the ordinary about him in everything he was and did, whether he wanted it or not, and he was alone and excluded from normal, respectable people, although he was certainly not a gypsy in a green caravan but the son of Consul Kröger, of the Kröger family... But why did Hans call him Tonio as long as they were alone, when, no sooner did a third person come along, than he began to feel embarrassed? Sometimes he was close to him. Sometimes he won him over. How did he betray him then, Tonio? He'd asked and taken his arm. But then, when Jimmerthal came along, he'd breathed a sigh of relief all the same. He'd put a distance between them and quite unnecessarily attacked him for his alien forename. How painful it was to be forced to see all this so clearly...! In the end Hans Hansen did like him a bit, when they were together. That he knew. But when a third person joined them he became embarrassed and sacrificed him. And he was alone again. He thought of King Philip. He thought of the King who wept...

'Heavens,' said Erwin Jimmerthal, 'now I really must get myself into town! So long, you two, and thanks for the fruit sweets!'

Whereupon he leapt up on a bench that stood beside the path, ran the length of it with his bandy legs and trotted off.

'I really like Jimmerthal,' said Hans emphatically. He had a self-confident, admirable way of announcing his preferences and dislikes, as if bestowing them from on high... and then he went back to talking about the riding lesson, picking up where he'd left off. Nor was it far to the house where Hans lived; the route along the ramparts didn't take long. They hung on to their caps and bowed their heads before the strong, damp wind that moaned and groaned in the leafless branches of the trees. And Hans Hansen talked, while Tonio only every now and again interposed a fake 'I see' and 'yes of course'. In fact Hans, carried away by what he had to say, had once more taken his arm, but Tonio experienced no pleasure, for it was only the illusion of closeness, quite insignificant.

So then they left the ramparts not far from the railway station, watched a train huff and puff its way past, trying to pick up speed, amused themselves by counting the number of carriages and waved to the man sitting wrapped in his fur coat high up in the last one of all. When they arrived at the Lindenplatz they stopped outside businessman Hansen's villa and Hans demonstrated in some detail what fun was to be had by standing on the bottom of the garden gate and swinging backwards and forwards on the hinges to make it squeak. But then he took his leave.

'I have to go in, really,' he said. 'So long, Tonio. Next time it will be me seeing you home, you can be sure of that.'

'So long, Hans,' said Tonio. 'It was nice to go for a walk.'

They shook hands—rather damp hands, damp and rusty from the garden gate. But when Hans looked into Tonio's eyes, something like a moment of conscience swept over his handsome face.

'I will read *Don Carlos*, by the way. Soon as I can,' he said all of a sudden. 'That bit with the King in his chamber must be topping!' Then he took his satchel under his arm and ran through the front garden. Before he disappeared inside he turned and nodded a last time.

And Tonio Kröger left that spot with his heart blazing and as if he had grown wings. The wind was behind him, but that was not the only reason he felt light as a feather.

Hans would read *Don Carlos*, and then they would have something between them that neither Jimmerthal nor anyone else could join in talking about! How well they understood each other! Who knows—perhaps next he could bring him to write poetry too?... No, no, he didn't want that. Hans shouldn't become like Tonio, only stay as he was, so fair and so strong. He should be just as everyone loved him and Tonio most of all! And yet it wouldn't go amiss if he read *Don Carlos*... And Tonio passed through the sturdy old gate, walked along the edge of the harbour and up the steep, draughty and wet gabled alleyway to his parents' house. His heart was alive; longing dwelt there and sadness and envy; a tiny bit of contempt; and a feeling of pure bliss.

2

When he was sixteen it was blonde Inge whom Tonio Kröger loved, Ingeborg Holm, who was the daughter of Doctor Holm, who lived on the marketplace where the tall Gothic fountain stood, with all its different pinnacles.

How did that happen? He'd seen her thousands of times; on one evening, however, he saw her in a certain light, saw how in conversation with a friend she had a certain exuberant way of laughing and leaning her head to one side, had a certain way of putting her hand, not particularly slender, definitely not what you would call a fine little girl's hand, to the back of her head, which caused the white gauze sleeves to draw up above her elbow; he heard how she stressed a word, it could have been any word, only that she hung on to it in a certain way, and spoke it with a particular burst of warmth in her voice; his heart was gripped with delight, and these feelings were much stronger than what he had felt from time to time when he gazed on Hans Hansen, when he was still a silly young boy.

That evening he took away with him an image of her, with her thick blonde hair, her smiling, almond-shaped blue eyes and the delicately understated patch of freckles across the bridge of her nose, couldn't get to sleep because he kept hearing the sound of her voice, tried softly to imitate the way she stressed this or that word—it didn't matter which—and he shivered. Experience taught him that this was love. But although he knew that love was bound to bring him a lot of pain, torment and humiliation, that it would destroy his peace of mind and fill his heart with more songs than it could bear and he would never find the tranquillity he needed to shape and finesse it into an artistic whole, still he accepted his feelings with joy, and abandoned himself wholly to nurturing it with his powers of mind; for, as he knew, love enriches people and brings them alive, and he longed to be enriched and alive, rather than remain unaffected, as he would need to, to achieve artistic perfection...

This occasion, when Tonio Kröger lost his heart to the happy, laughing Ingeborg Holm, happened in the drawing room of Frau Husteede, Consul Husteede's wife, who that evening had moved the furniture aside to host a dancing lesson. It was a course of private instruction in which only members of the best families took part, and they gathered successively in their parents' houses in order to learn dancing and etiquette. To this end ballet master Knaak came expressly from Hamburg every week.

François Knaak was his name, and what a man he was! '*J'ai l'honneur de me vous représenter*,' he said. 'May I have the honour of introducing myself? My name, *mon nom*, is Knaak... and one doesn't say this when one is bowing but when one has straightened up again—and one speaks with restraint but still clearly. It will not be required every day to have to introduce oneself in French, but if it is done in the correct language and without blemish it will also considerably enhance one's performance in German.' How marvellously snugly his silken black tailcoat fitted his plump hips! His trousers fell in gentle folds on to his patent shoes, these made fancy with broad satin ribbons, and his brown eyes gazed tired and happy, as if contented with their own beauty round about...

Anyone would have been impressed by his excess of confidence and decorum. He walked up to the lady of the house—and I have to say no one walked as he did, swaying and sashaying, with an elastic, majestic step—bowed, and waited for a hand to be extended in his direction. Receiving it, he quietly expressed his thanks, moved backwards with featherlight steps, turned on his left foot, propelling his right, with the toe pointed, sideways across the floor and withdrew, his hips swaying...

It was proper to walk backwards, bowing, towards the door, whenever one exited from polite society, it was never right to pull up a chair, taking it by the leg or sliding it along the floor. Oh no! One walked over and picked it up by the arms and then set it down again noiselessly. While standing, one never folded one's arms across one's chest, nor pushed one's tongue into the corner of one's mouth; were it to happen nevertheless, well then Herr Knaak had a way of doing the same which ensured that one would be revolted by such behaviour for the rest of one's life...

This was decorum. In the matter of dancing, meanwhile, it's possible that Herr Knaak was its master to an even higher degree. In the spacious salon where the chandeliers burnt bright with gas flames and there were candles on the mantelpiece, the floor was strewn with talcum powder and the pupils—*les élèves*—stood in a semicircle not saying a word. On the other side of the curtain, in the adjoining room, sat the mothers and the aunts, in red plush armchairs, and regarded Herr Knaak through their lorgnettes. He was leaning forwards, using two fingers to pluck up the tails of his morning coat either side, ready to demonstrate on his featherlight feet the individual steps of the mazurka. If, however, what he really intended was to blind his public with his sheer ability, he achieved it, for suddenly and for no compelling reason he propelled himself from the ground, twirling his legs in the air with astonishing rapidity. He executed what a singer would call a trill, and then with a muted plop that astonished the assembled company returned to Earth...

'What kind of ape that is I can't fathom,' thought Tonio Kröger after his fashion. But he could see that Inge Holm, the happy, laughing Ingeborg Holm, often had a smile on her face that she was unaware of as she followed Herr Knaak's movements, and it was not only this that brought Tonio to feel in his heart something like admiration for such miraculously controlled physicality. How calm and focused on the task Herr Knaak's eyes looked! They didn't stare their way into things, to the point where everything became complicated and sad; all they knew was that they were themselves brown and beautiful. But why did he hold himself in such a proud fashion? You'd have to be brainless to be able to move like him; but then you'd be loved. You would be lovable. Tonio noticed that Inge, sweet, blonde Inge, was following Herr Knaak with her eyes and understood all too well why she was doing it. Would a girl ever look at him like that?

But yes, that happened. Step forward Magdalena Vermehren, Solicitor Vermehren's daughter, with her soft lips and her big, dark, shining eyes full of seriousness and dreaming. She often fell over when they were dancing; but when it was time for the Ladies' Choice she came over to him, she knew he wrote poetry, she'd twice asked him to show her his poems, and often she looked at him from far off with lowered head. But what was it to him? He loved Inge Holm, blonde Inge who was always laughing and happy, who surely held him in contempt because he wrote poetic things... he looked upon her, upon her narrow, almond-shaped blue eyes, which were full of merriment and mockery, and a feeling of longing and envy, a bitter, insistent pain, that she would always exclude him and he would forever remain a stranger to her, invaded his heart and began to burn...

'First pair *en avant*!' said Herr Knaak, asking for the first pair to come forward, and no words can convey how superbly this man pronounced that nasal 'n'. They were practising the quadrille, and to Tonio's deep shock he found himself in one and the same square as Inge Holm. He avoided her as far as he could but the dance kept bringing him back close to her; he shielded his eyes from approaching her, but one way or another he was always looking at her... now here she was hand in hand with red-headed Ferdinand Matthiessen, gliding and stepping past him, now throwing her head back and, breathing a sigh of relief, taking up a place opposite him. Herr Heinzelmann, the pianist, reached for the keys with his bony hands, Herr Knaak gave the order, and the quadrille began.

She moved in front of him, back and forth, this way and that way, stepping here and turning there; a scent hung in the air from

24

her hair or from the delicate white fabric of her dress; sometimes she touched him, and his eyes became ever dimmer. I love you, dear sweet Inge, he said to himself, and he charged those words with all the pain he felt that she was so much enjoying the dance, relishing it so much that she took no notice of him. A marvellous poem of Storm's came back to him: 'I want to sleep, but you must dance.' The humiliating absurdity tormented him, to have to dance whereas one was in love...

'First pair *en avant!*' said Herr Knaak, as a new set began. '*Compliment! Moulinet des dames! Tour de main!*', which was to say 'Greet your partners, Ladies' Mill, and round you go!' And no one can convey the elegant manner in which the dance teacher swallowed the silent 'e' in 'de'.

'Second pair *en avant!*' It was the turn of Tonio Kröger and his lady. '*Compliment!*' And Tonio bowed. '*Moulinet des dames!*' And Tonio Kröger, with his head lowered and his brow dark, placed his hand on the hands of the four ladies, on the hand of Inge Holm, and danced, maypole-fashion, the '*moulinet*'.

People around started giggling and laughing. Herr Knack took up his ballet position, which was a stylized way of expressing his outrage. 'Oh dear!' he cried. 'Stop, stop! Kröger has got in with the women! *En arrière*, Fräulein Kröger, back you go! *Fi donc*, for shame!' He addressed him as a girl. 'Everyone understood it except you. Quick! Quick as you can! Back you go!' And he pulled out a yellow silk handkerchief and shooed him along with it, back to his place.

Just about everyone laughed, the boys, the girls and the women on the far side of the curtain, for Herr Knack had turned the incident into something very amusing, and people found it entertaining as they would in the theatre. Only Herr Heinzelmann was waiting with an unamused, businesslike look on his face, for he was inured to Herr Knaak's posturing.

So the quadrille continued. And then it was the interval. With a clink the kitchen-maid entered through the door with a tray of wine jelly glasses and the cook followed in her wake with a plateful of English fruitcake. But Tonio stole away, escaping secretly into the corridor, and stood with his hands behind his back in front of a window with the blind pulled down, without thinking that one couldn't see anything through the blind, and so it was absurd to stand there and pretend to be looking out.

But he was looking inside himself, where there was so much torment and so much longing. Why was he here? Why? Why was he not sitting in his room at the window and reading Storm's *Immensee*, and looking out into the evening garden from time to time, where the old walnut tree groaned under its own weight? That would have been his place. Let the others dance and do it energetically and be good at it...! But no, no, his place was here, where he knew himself to be near Inge, even if he was standing alone and trying from afar, in the buzz of glasses clinking and people laughing, to distinguish her voice, which resonated with so much warm life. Your almond-shaped, laughing blue eyes, my blonde Inge! The only way to be beautiful and gay like you is not to read *Immensee* and never to do anything of the kind; that is the sad thing...!

Surely she would come his way! Surely she must have noticed that he'd gone, must feel how it was for him, was bound to follow him, even if only out of pity, put her hand on his shoulder and say: come back inside with us, be happy, I love you. And he listened behind him and waited tensely, although it wasn't a sensible thing to do; he just wished her to come. But of course she didn't come. That kind of thing doesn't happen on Earth.

Did she laugh at him, just like all the others? Yes, she did, however much he would have wanted to deny it, for her sake and his. The problem was he had only danced the *moulinet des dames* because he was so absorbed by her presence. Who gives a fig? One day they would perhaps stop laughing. Hadn't it happened recently that a magazine had accepted one of his poems, only to go bankrupt before the poem could appear? The day would come when he was famous, and everything he wrote would be published, and well then we'll see if that doesn't make an impression on Inge Holm... But it would *not* make an impression on her, that was the truth of it. Yes it would impress Magdalene Vermehren, who was always falling over. But never Inge Holm, never blue-eyed, laughing, happy Inge. So wasn't it therefore pointless?...

Tonio shuddered painfully at the thought. To feel that you have these wonderful powers within, shaped by melancholy, powers of imagination to play with this and conjure that, and at the same time to know that those you long to be among have no interest, that what you can do means nothing to them, that hurts a great deal. But although he stood alone, excluded and without hope in front of a closed blind, and in his distress was pretending he could see through it, he was still happy. For his heart was alive then. Warmly and sadly it beat for you, Ingeborg Holm, and his soul embraced your blonde, bright, extravagantly ordinary little personality in a blessed moment of self-renunciation.

More than once he stood with a flushed face in some lonely place, where music and the smell of flowers and the sound of glasses clinking was faintly detectable in the distance, and tried to discern in the distant hum of the party your ringing voice, stood there in pain because of you and was nevertheless happy. More than once it made him feel ill that he could talk to Magdalene Vermehren, who was always falling over, that she understood him and laughed with him and was serious with him while his blonde Inge, even if he sat next to her, seemed distant and foreign and as if he were driving her away, for the language he spoke was not hers; and still he was happy. For happiness, he told himself, is not to be loved; that is a sop to one's vanity, and mixed with disgust. Happiness is to love someone and perhaps to arrange tricky little ways of sometimes coming closer to the beloved. And he made an inward note of this thought, digested it thoroughly and experienced it in the depths of his heart.

To be faithful! Tonio thought. I want to be faithful and to love you, Ingeborg, for as long as I live. He so much wanted the best. And yet he heard a whisper inside him, inspiring a faint fear and mournfulness, telling him that he'd already completely forgotten Hans Hansen, even though he saw him every day. And it was an ugly and pitiful fact that this soft and rather spiteful voice was right, that time would pass and days arrive when Tonio was no longer so absolutely ready to die for the happy, laughing Inge as he once was, because he felt in himself both the desire and the power to achieve some remarkable things in the world in his own fashion.

He hovered gingerly around the sacrificial altar on which the pure and chaste flame of his love was flickering, knelt before it and sheltered it and nurtured it in every way, because he wanted to be faithful. And yet with time, unnoticed, without any noise or fuss, it went out all the same.

Tonio Kröger went on standing a while longer in front of the extinguished flame, full of astonishment and disappointment that faithfulness on Earth was not possible. But then he shrugged his shoulders and went on his way.

3

He went the way he had to go, unevenly, not paying proper attention, whistling to himself, with his head on one side looking out into the distance, and if he went wrong, then it happened because for a good number of people there is no right way. Had anyone asked him what in the world he hoped to become, they would have received different answers, for it was his habit to say (and he had already written it down) that he bore within himself a thousand possible ways of existing, together with the secret awareness that in actual fact they were all complete impossibilities...

Even before he left his close-walled native town, the ties that bound him to it, the connecting threads, had quietly begun to loosen. The old Kröger family was gradually descending into a state where it was in decline and falling apart, and people had every reason to count Tonio Kröger's own person and his way of being as one of the indications of that state. His father's mother, the head of the tribe, had died, and not long after that his father—that tall, thoughtful, immaculately dressed gentleman with the poppy in his buttonhole—followed. The grand house of the Krögers, along with all its worthy history, was put up for sale, and the firm closed down. Tonio's mother, however, his beautiful, fiery mother who played the piano and the mandolin so wonderfully and for whom nothing mattered much, everything was pretty much all the same to her, married again after a period of a year, and not just anyone: she married a musician who was a virtuoso with an Italian name and she followed him to somewhere far away under a blue sky. Tonio Kröger found this not quite in order; but was it for *him* to tell her she ought to have reconsidered? He wrote poetry and couldn't even answer the question of what he thought of becoming when he was older...

And he left his home town, with all its tight little corners and angles, and where a damp wind blew around the gables, left the fountain and the old walnut tree in the garden, the things that had been dear to him in his youth, left the sea too, which he loved, and did so without pain. For he'd become clever and grown up, and had grasped how it had formed a context for him, and he was full of contempt for the humble, artless existence that had kept him in its midst for so long.

He devoted himself to the power that seemed to him the most sublime on Earth, into whose service he felt called, and which promised him achievement and honours, the power of the intellect and of the written word, which from its throne looked down with a smile on unreflective, inarticulate life. With all the passion of his youth he devoted himself to the power of the word, and it rewarded him with everything it had to give and mercilessly took from him everything it was accustomed to ask for in return.

It sharpened his eye, and enabled him to see through the big words that inflate men's chests. It opened up to him the souls of others, and also his own. It turned him into a seer and showed him what lay within and showed him what things were final, underlying all the words and the deeds. But what he actually saw was this: comedy and misery—comedy and misery.

With the torment and the arrogance of these insights loneliness came upon him, because the circles in which harmless people moved had no place for a young man with his sense of joy and darkness, and the mark on his forehead disturbed them. Meanwhile his love of words, and of artistic form, grew ever sweeter, for as he liked to say (and had already written down), insight into the human plight would make us unfailingly wretched, if the joys of expression did not keep us awake and give us a task ...

He lived in cities, and in the south, where the sun promised to ripen his language more luxuriantly; and perhaps it was the blood of his mother which drew him there. But because his heart was dead and without love, so he had many adventures of the flesh, descended into lust and burning shame and suffered beyond words. Perhaps it was what he had inherited from his father, that tall, thoughtful, immaculately dressed gentleman with a poppy in his buttonhole, that made him suffer so much in the south and sometimes awakened a weak memory of and a longing for the pleasures of the soul, which had once been his own, and which wherever lust led him he could not find again.

A hatred and disgust of everything sensual gripped him and a great thirst for purity and respectability and peace, at the same time as he breathed in the air of art, warmish and sweet, pregnant with the perfume of a continuous spring, in which the secret, raging creative process ferments and germinates its way in an ecstasy of making new life. And so it came about that, helplessly thrown back and forth between two crass extremes, between an icy intellectualism and a burning sensuality that was devouring him, plagued by his conscience, he led an exhausting life, which he, Tonio Kröger, basically despised. I've so much chosen the wrong path, he thought every now and again. How is it possible for me to find myself caught up in all these eccentric adventures? After all, I'm not a gypsy in a green caravan, not given the family I come from…

But, to the degree that his health suffered, his artistic practice improved, became selective, lofty, exquisite, discerning, irritably opposed to all that was banal and tremendously demanding in questions of pitch and taste. The first time he was on stage there came great applause and delight from people who knew what he was about, for it was a finely crafted piece of work he had delivered, full of humour and an awareness of human sadness. His name, the same name which his schoolmasters had used to call him forward and rebuke him, the same name with which he had signed his first poems to the walnut tree, the fountain and the sea, this composite of sounds from south and north, this patrician German name with a touch of the exotic about it, became a sign of excellence, for entailed in the painful details of his personal experience was a rare stubbornness and an unstinting application, as he dreamt of prizes; and as the energy he brought to his writing struggled with the irritable, fastidious choices he insisted on making in matters of taste, so unusual work emerged from his terrible torment.

He worked not like someone who works in order to live but like someone who wants nothing else but to work, because he thinks nothing of himself as a living person and only wants to be judged in terms of what he creates, and all the time goes about grey and inconspicuous, like an actor with his make-up removed, who is nothing so long as he is not playing a role. He worked silently, isolated, invisibly and utterly despising small minds for whom talent was a social ornament, and who, whether they were rich or poor, whether they went about wild and dressed in rags or indulged themselves in the finery of silk ties, basically were people who were minded to live happy, lovable and cultured lives, unaware that good work only arises from the pressure of a bad life, that living means not working, and that one must die in order to be a perfect creator.

4

'Am I disturbing you?' asked Tonio Kröger in the doorway of the studio. He held his hat in his hand and even bowed a fraction, even though Lisaveta Ivanovna was his friend, to whom he said everything.

'Don't stand on ceremony, Tonio Kröger, do yourself a good turn and just come in!' she answered, making the German syllables bounce, as was her wont. 'Everyone knows you had a good upbringing and know how to behave.' As she spoke she moved the brush to the palette in her left hand, held out her right to him and with a laugh and a shake of her head stared into his face.

'I see you're working,' he said. 'Let me see… oh, you've made progress.' And he contemplated alternately the coloured sketches that were leaning on chairs either side of the easel and the big canvas, with a squared-off grid over it, on which, in the smudgy, schematic charcoal outline, the first specks of colour were starting to appear.

It was in Munich, in a building several storeys high behind the Schellingstraße. Outside, seen through the wide north-facing window, there was nothing but blue sky, twittering birds and sunshine, and the young, sweet breath of spring wafting in through an open skylight mingled with the smell of fixative and oil paint which filled the large atelier. Nothing stopped the golden light of a bright afternoon flooding the extensive bareness of the room, uninhibitedly illuminating the rather damaged floor, the table under the window covered with little bottles, tubes and brushes and the unframed studies on the paperless walls; nothing stopped the light illuminating a screen made of raw silk that closed off a stylishly furnished corner for living and relaxing, illuminating too the work in progress on the easel and the painter and the writer standing in front of it.

She was about his age, that is, a bit over thirty. In her dark-blue overall, flecked with paint, she sat on a low stool and rested her chin on her hand. Her brown hair, tightly curled and already a little greying at the sides, covered her temples in soft waves and framed her face. She was a brunette, with Slav features, her face with its snub nose, prominent cheekbones and small black shining eyes infinitely charming. Focused, sceptical and at the same time as if excited, she cast a sharp, narrowed critical eye over her work…

He was standing beside her, resting his right hand on his hip and with his left giving a quick tug on his brown beard. His angular eyebrows were dark and in motion, as if he was making some effort, and at the same time he whistled softly, as usual. He was most elegantly, indeed immaculately dressed, in a classically tailored soft-grey suit. But his finely wrought brow, over which his dark hair was strikingly simply and neatly combed, showed signs of a nervous tic, and the features of his chiselled southern face had grown sharp, as if a sculptor had worked to enhance them, while at the same time the outline of his mouth was so soft, his chin so weakly formed... After a while he passed a hand over his brow and eyes and turned aside.

'I shouldn't have come,' he said.

'Why shouldn't you have, Tonio Kröger?'

'I've just got up from my work, Lisaveta, and in my head it looks just like this canvas looks. A framework, a pale, messy sketch full of corrections, a spot of colour here and there, nothing else; and now I come here and see the same thing. I find the same intractable conflicts here', he said, and sniffed the air, 'that plague me at home. It's a strange thing. If a thought preoccupies you then you find it cropping up everywhere, you can even smell it on the wind. Fixative and the scent of spring, isn't that it? Art and—oh yes, what's the other thing? Don't say "nature", Lisaveta, "nature" doesn't capture it. Dear me no, I'd have done better to go for a walk, although the question remains, had I done so would I have felt better? Five minutes ago, not far from here, I met a colleague, Adelbert. He writes novels. "God damn the spring," he said in his aggressive style. "It's the most awful time of year and so it always will be! Can you form a single sensible thought, Kröger, can you work up a single sequence in your writing where you make your point and carry it through? How can you do that when your blood is racing indecently and you're troubled by a whole heap of inappropriate feelings, which, no sooner have you examined them, turn out to be the most incredibly trivial stuff: feelings that are on a par with the chrysalis that doesn't turn into a butterfly, or doesn't turn into anything at all. You can't put them to any use. As for me, I'm heading for a café. That's neutral territory. Cafés aren't touched by the changing of the seasons, as you know. They keep themselves at a distance. They stand for the sublime sphere of literature, and only there can one produce superior ideas…" And he went into a café; and perhaps I should have gone with him.'

Lisaveta looked amused.

'That's good, Tonio Kröger. I like that stuff about "when your blood is racing indecently". And your friend is right in a way, spring is not the best time to work. But please note, that doesn't stop me working up this little thing here, which will make its little point and have its effect, as Adelbert would say. Afterwards we'll go into my "salon" and have a cup of tea, and you can tell me everything; I mean I can see that today you need to talk. Until that moment dump yourself somewhere, you could sit on that box over there, if you're not worried about your fine clothes…'

'Oh, don't go on about my clothes, Lisaveta Ivanovna! I could go about in a torn velvet jacket or a red silk waistcoat: is that what you want? As an artist the adventures going on inside oneself are surely enough. Outwardly one should dress properly, for heaven's sake, and behave like a decent person… no, it's not that I need to talk,' he said, and watched her mixing colours on her palette. 'What you can hear is that I have a problem, conflicting thoughts, on my mind, which stop me working… So what were we talking about just now? Ah yes about Adelbert, the novelist, and what a proud and unshakeable man he is. "Spring is the most awful time of year," he said, and went into a café. You have to know what you want, don't you? I mean spring makes me anxious too. I too get confused by all the feelings it awakens in me, silly but glorious memories; what I don't manage is to blame the spring, and to cast it aside in disdain; and that's because I am ashamed of myself in its presence; its purity, its naturalness, its triumphant youth all make me feel ashamed. And I don't know whether I should envy or think less of Adelbert, because he knows nothing of any of this...

'Certainly one doesn't work well in spring, and why? Because one is full of feelings. And because it's only someone who's got no idea about the matter who thinks that a creative person needs to have feelings. Every genuine and truthful artist has to smile at the naivety of a philistine assumption like that—it may make him sad to admit it, but such naivety still makes him smile. For what one says can never be the main thing, it's just the raw material, in and of itself neither here nor there. The aesthetic object is made of that material, but shaped in tranquillity, like a game played with it. The aesthetic object happens when the artist can manipulate his materials and be their master. If what you have to say matters to you too much, if it makes your heart beat warmly, you can be sure that the result will be a complete fiasco. You will be pathetic, you will be sentimental. You'll look like a fool trying to be serious. Something clumsy, out of control, lacking in irony and piquancy, boring and banal will come into being in your hands, and nothing but other people's indifference, nothing but disappointment and misery for you as the artist, will be the outcome... That's how it is, Lisaveta: feelings, warm, heartfelt emotions, are always banal and unusable, and artistically they are just the irritations and cold ecstasies of our ruined artists' nerves. It's necessary to be something inhuman and beyond human, to stand in a strangely distant relationship to the human, not to get involved, to be in a position, and even for a moment tempted, to turn humanity into a game, and to play that game until you can present it effectively and with the right artistic finesse. To have talent in matters of style, form and choice of words already presupposes this cool and discerning attitude towards all things human; indeed it presupposes a certain human impoverishment and desolation. For strong, healthy emotions don't make for finesse, that's the long and the short of it. It's over for an artist when he becomes a real, feeling person. That's what Adelbert knew when he took himself off to a café, when he escaped into "the sublime sphere of literature". Absolutely right!'

'The Lord be with him, *batushka*,' said Lisaveta, and washed her hands in a tin bowl. 'You don't need to follow him, my dear German friend.'

'No, Lisaveta, I won't be following him, and for the sole and single reason that now and again I am still capable of feeling a little ashamed of being an artist, still capable of having spring make me feel that way. You know, I sometimes receive letters from strangers, people praising me and thanking me for my work, letters full of admiration from a readership my work has touched. I read their missives and I'm moved to tears that my art has evoked such warm and clumsy human feelings, I feel a kind of pity for so much naïve enthusiasm, as it speaks out of their words, and I blush at the thought of the sobering shock this upright person would get, could they see behind the scenes, if in their innocence they could ever understand that a decent, healthy, proper person just doesn't go in for writing, miming, composing... all of which doesn't stop me using their admiration for my genius to give myself a boost and stimulate new ideas. I take their admiration terribly seriously, and end up making a face like a monkey playing the role of a great man... Oh, Lisaveta, don't make me listen to your objections! I tell you I am often exhausted by the business of portraying humanity without being part of it. It makes me want to die... Is the artist a man at all? Maybe we should ask "womankind" for the answer! It seems to me we artists all share a bit the fate of those papal singers who have been operated on... we sing beautifully and movingly. Even so—'

'You ought to be a bit ashamed of yourself, Tonio Kröger. Come and have a cup of tea. The water will boil in a minute, and help yourself to one of these *papyrosy*. Where had you got to before I offered you a Russian cigarette? I know, you were talking about singing the soprano part even though you're a man. Do go on. But feel a little ashamed of yourself all the same. If I didn't know of the pride and passion and commitment you bring to your profession...'

'Don't speak of any "profession", Lisaveta Ivanovna! Literature's not a profession, it's a curse—just so you know. When do you first feel this curse? Early on, terribly early. At a time when you ought still to be living in peace and harmony with God and the world. You begin to feel yourself branded as puzzlingly different from everyone else, puzzlingly different from how normal, decent people are, and the gulf of feeling that divides you from other people, all the irony and unbelief you nurture inside you, all your contrary opinions and deep insight, this gulf gapes ever wider, you are alone, and from here on there is no way of making yourself understood. What a fate! Supposing that the artist's heart has retained enough life, that it has remained sufficiently *loving*, it's frightful to experience...! Your self-consciousness becomes enflamed, because you can be among thousands of people and still feel, still be aware of this mark on your brow that no one can fail to see. I knew an actor of genius who as a person had to wrestle with a painful awkwardness and insecurity. His inflamed sense of himself, on the occasions he had no role to play, when his art didn't require him to represent another person, had a terrible effect on this consummate artist and impoverished man... An artist, a real artist, not someone whose middle-class profession is art but someone predestined and condemned to being an artist, you can spot a mile away in a crowd. That feeling of being cut off and not belonging, of being recognized and observed for what they are, something at once regal and embarrassed is on their face. In the features of a prince who puts on ordinary clothes and walks through a crowd of commoners you can observe something similar. But a set of ordinary clothes is not going to help here, Lisaveta! You can disguise yourself, bury yourself in other clothes, you can dress like a diplomat or a lieutenant of the guards on holiday: you will hardly need to open your eyes and speak a word and everyone will know that you're not a person like they are, but something alien, something that drives people away, something other...

'But *what* is an artist? No question has produced more lasting answers vis-à-vis a humanity that likes to feel comfortable with itself and can only bear so much reality. "Well you know it's a gift," good people say modestly when they feel an artist's power, and because in their well-intentioned opinion amusing and sublime effects must most certainly have amusing and sublime causes, so no one suspects that the gift in question is extremely nasty, extremely questionable... One knows that artists are easily offended—one also knows that it's not common to find this kind of behaviour among people of good conscience and with a firm sense of themselves... You see, Lisaveta, I have in the depths of my soul—translated into the terms of the intellect—this wholesale suspicion of artists as a type, the kind of suspicion that any of my ancestors, back up north in that town with the narrow streets, that any of the generations of my family who were always so unshakeable in their sense of their own decency, would have brought to any travelling entertainer and any artiste taking his chance, had they entered his house. I know a banker, a grey-haired businessman, who has a gift for writing short stories. He makes use of this gift when he has a few hours to spare, and what he produces is sometimes excellent. Despite this—and I do say "despite"—sublime endowment of nature this man is not wholly blameless; on the contrary, he has already been punished with a loss of freedom in the past, for good reason. Indeed it was actually only in prison that he became aware of what he could do, and it's his experiences as a convict that form the basis of all he writes. One could, if one were bold enough, draw the conclusion that one has to feel at home in some kind of penal institution in order to become a writer. But surely the suspicion arises that his experiences in gaol are less intimately connected with the roots and sources of his artistic practice compared with *whatever brought him there in the first place*—? A banker who has a poetic gift, who can write stories, is quite a rarity, don't you think? But a blameless banker, a pillar of society, who writes stories and who is not a criminal—*that just can't happen*… Fine, so you're laughing now, but I'm only half joking. There's no problem, no problem in the world more tormenting than that of art, the artist and their effect among people. Take the wondrous achievement of an artist at his most typical and therefore most powerful, take such a morbid and deeply ambivalent work as *Tristan and Isolde* and observe the effect it has on healthy young people with an outstandingly normal way of experiencing things. You can see how they are uplifted and the experience is intense. They feel warmth and enthusiasm of the right kind. They may even be tempted to contemplate their own "artistic" project… They are good people, but dilettantes! To us artists it looks completely different, nothing to do with the dreams of folk with warm hearts and "real enthusiasm". I've seen artists mobbed by women, and by young people, they give them such great joy, it's a triumph, and all the while *I* knew what those artists were about… In what concerns the origins, the side effects and the conditions of art and artistry, one keeps coming across the most curious new findings…'

'In others, Tonio Kröger—forgive me—or not only in others?'

He said nothing. He frowned, drawing his angular eyebrows together, and whistled.

'Give me your cup, Tonio. The tea's not strong. And help yourself to another cigarette. Let me just say that, as you know very well, you see things in a way that isn't necessarily how they have to be seen…'

'That's Horatio's answer, dear Lisaveta. "'Twere to consider too curiously, to consider so." Well, isn't it?'

'All I'm saying is that one could just as easily see things from another angle, Tonio Kröger. I'm just a silly woman who paints, but if I have any answer to give you, if I can for a moment protect your profession a little from yourself, I will. I'm sure that nothing I say will be new, just a warning, of which you yourself are perfectly aware… along these lines: to see literature as having a sacred, purifying effect, to see the passions as undone by the truth of the written word, to see literature as a way to understanding, love and forgiveness, to grasp the redeeming power of language, to see the literary mind as the most noble manifestation of the human intellect generally, to see the writer as a perfect human being, as a saint—would you say that to see things *that way* would be not to look at them closely enough?'

'You of all people have a right to speak like that, Lisaveta Ivanovna, thinking of the work of your writers, thinking of the Russian literature that we all worship, which is indeed holy, just as you say. But I'm not ignoring your objections, no indeed, they're part of what's burdening me here today… Look at me, I don't look particularly happy, do I? A bit old and drawn and tired, don't you think? But to come back to that ability to see truth, that's what a person might feel who is naturally inclined to think the best, someone tender-minded, ready to believe in things and a little bit sentimental, and who, if they were given psychological insight, would be destroyed, set on a path of no return; to observe, to take note of even the most tormenting things, and remain spiritually buoyant, in full awareness of the superiority that the civilized moral life brings over the disgusting inventions of raw being—oh, yes, I give you that! Only sometimes, despite all the pleasure you take in getting the words right, the whole thing can overwhelm you. To understand everything is to forgive everything? I really don't know. There is something, Lisaveta, that I call the deepest revulsion: when you don't want to know what lies beneath things, and if you do know you can never be reconciled to that insight and death will fill your thoughts—the case of Hamlet the Dane, the typical man of literature. He knew full well what it was to be called to a true knowledge of things without being born to it. To keep one's eyes wide open even when they are full of heartfelt tears, to understand, to take note, to observe and with a smile store up those observations for the future, to do all that even in a moment when hands are finding each other, lips are meeting, when the human gaze is so dazzled with intense feeling it can no longer see at all—it's a curse, Lisaveta, it drags you down, you feel outrage... but to feel outrage doesn't help.

'Another no less charming aspect of the matter is of course when people get tired and blasé, and can only approach truth indifferently and ironically. That's the case with intellectuals, who've given up, who are completely devoid of hope and just stand there in silence. They've been through it all, they've seen everything. The idea of truth is old and tedious. You may have made an effort to establish that something is true, and perhaps as a young person you may feel a certain joy at having done so, and they will answer your banal enlightenment with a snort... Oh dear, I'm afraid so, literature makes people tired, Lisaveta. Believe me, society can be like that. People are so sceptical and so averse to having an opinion that they take you for an idiot for expressing one, when actually you are only high-minded and disappointed that you can't do anything. That's what I have to say about "truth". As for "the power of the word", there perhaps it's more a matter of a way of turning emotions into coldness, putting feelings on ice, rather than some kind of spiritual delivery? Seriously, "the power of the word" has an icy and appalling relevance when it comes to this hasty and superficial parcelling-up of emotion by means of literary language. Is your heart overflowing, has some sweet or sublime experience taken hold of you to an excessive degree? Nothing could be simpler! Go and see a "man of letters" and everything will be sorted out for you in the shortest time. He will analyse and find a way of formulating what you've been through, he'll give it a name and put it into a language where it can be talked about, he'll look after it for you once and for all, it won't worry you any more, and he won't accept thanks. You on the other hand can go back home feeling relieved, calm and collected, and wonder quite what it was that plunged you into such sweet urgency. And you want seriously to speak up for this cold, vain charlatan? His credo is that once something is put into words it's dealt with. Put the whole world into words and you can call it done with, solved, sorted... that's very good! But I'm not a nihilist...'[1]

'You're not what—' said Lisaveta, who was just lifting her spoonful of tea to her lips and froze in that position.

'Fine... yes, I know... but what I mean is, Lisaveta, that I'm not such a person when it comes to people's vital emotions, that's what I'm saying. You see, these writers whom I call "men of letters" basically don't understand Life: don't grasp that Life actually cares to go on living, that it isn't ashamed of itself, even after it's been "put into words" and "dealt with". Literature may think it redeems Life, but Life just carries on sinning. The "men of letters" don't understand because from their intellectual point of view all action, all engagement with Life, is sinful…'

'I've almost finished, Lisaveta. Hear me out. I love Life—that's a confession. Take it from me and put it somewhere for safekeeping. I've never made it to anyone before. People have said it and they've even written and published it, that either I hate life or fear it or despise it or find it repugnant. I enjoy hearing that; it flatters me; but that doesn't make it any more accurate. I love Life, you're smiling, Lisaveta, and I know why. Don't think of Cesare Borgia or of some intoxicated philosophy which marches under his name![2] This Cesare Borgia is nothing to me, has not a jot of significance, and I'll never ever understand how anyone can revere what is exceptional and demonic as some kind of ideal. No, Life, as it stands in everlasting contradiction to intellect, and to art, Life is not a vision of blood-spattered heroism and savage beauty, it is not what presents itself to us out-of-the-ordinary folk as out of the ordinary; rather it's what is normal, respectable and lovable that is the object of our longing. I long for Life in all its seductive banality! Anyone whose ultimate and deepest enthusiasm is for the refined, eccentric and satanic, who doesn't grasp what it means to yearn for harmless, simple things embedded in everyday life, anyone who doesn't yearn for a little friendship, devotion, familiarity and human happiness is not an artist by a long chalk. It's all about a surreptitious yearning for the bliss of ordinariness, Lisaveta, and being consumed by that yearning…!

'A human friend! Can you believe how proud and happy it would make me to possess a friend among the human race? Until now all I've known have been demons, bogeymen, profoundly unwholesome types and wraiths who've renounced truth, that is, my friends have been writers.

'Sometimes I find myself on a platform somewhere, facing people in a room who have come to listen to me. And do you know what happens to me, I watch myself looking at the rows of faces, catch myself looking about the room, with a question weighing on my conscience, namely, who are these people who have come to see me, who are applauding me and thanking me, people my art has brought me into a kind of ideal contact with... And I can't find what I'm looking for. I find the herd and the community, which I know very well, like a gathering of early Christians; people with clumsy bodies and fine souls, people who are always tripping over, so to say, you understand what I'm getting at, and whose poetry is a gentle revenge on Life—the people in the audience are always just the ones in some difficulty, people longing for what they don't have, poor people, and there's never a representative of the others, you know, Lisaveta, the blue-eyed types who don't need the intellectual life...!

'And wouldn't it be pathetically inconsistent to hope that it might be different? It makes no sense, to love Life and yet to strive with all one's capacities to draw it over to one's own side, to capture it for refinement and melancholy, to put it to the service of noble, sickly literature. The realm of Art is growing, and health and innocence are diminishing on Earth. Whatever is left of these we must preserve at all costs, and we shouldn't try to seduce with poetry people who would far rather be browsing in books about horses, looking at the pictures of them in motion!

'For, in the end, what would look more pathetic than Life trying its hand with Art? We artists have no greater contempt than for dilettantes, which is to say, for normal, vital people who think they might like one day to become an artist as well. I can assure you that this kind of contempt belongs within my own personal experience. I'm somewhere in company in a grand house, people are eating, drinking and chatting, getting on just fine, and I feel happy and grateful to be able to disappear for a while among harmless upright people, as if I were one of them. Suddenly (and this really happened to me) an officer stands up, a lieutenant, a good-looking, well-built man standing tall and straight, whose ceremonial uniform would never have led me to believe he was capable of such an indiscretion, and without beating about the bush asks if he may read out a poem he has written. People smile with dismay and say of course, and he carries out his intention, reading from a piece of paper he had been hiding in his lap until that moment, something about music and love, in short, terribly deep and completely ineffectual. For heaven's sake! A lieutenant! A man of the world! He really didn't need to do that…! And what happens is what is bound to happen: long faces, silence, a little bit of forced applause and general discomfort all around. The first reaction I become conscious of inside myself is that I feel jointly guilty for the disturbance this thoughtless young man has caused among the guests; and, can you imagine, because it's my *métier* he's botched, people give me scornful and frosty looks too. The second thing is that this person, towards whose whole being I had just now felt the greatest respect, suddenly falls in my estimation, down, down, down… I wish him well. I pity him. I go up to him like a few other kindly and well-meaning gentlemen and have a word with him. 'My congratulations, Herr Leutnant!', I say. 'What a beguiling gift you have! Really that was exquisite!' And I come close to patting him on the shoulder. But is to wish him well the right reaction one should offer to a lieutenant? He made a mistake! He stood there and was made to pay for his error with great embarrassment. He didn't understand that you cannot pluck a tiny leaf, even one, from the laurel bush of Art without paying for it with your life. There I'm of one mind with my colleague, the criminal banker. But do you not find, Lisaveta, that I'm talking non-stop today, just like Hamlet?'

'Have you finished, Tonio Kröger?'

'No. But I won't go on.'

'Good. It's enough. Would you like an answer?'

'Do you have one?'

'I think I have. I've listened to you very carefully, Tonio, from start to finish, and I will give you an answer that fits everything you've said this afternoon, and which is the solution to the problem that's been bothering you so much. Here it is! The answer is that you are, even as you sit there, simply a bourgeois. You belong to the middle class.'

'Can that be?' he asked, and sank back a little into himself...

'You find that hard to take, don't you, and that's how it should be. That's why I'm going to soften my verdict a little, I can do that. You're a middle-class man who's taken the wrong path, Tonio Kröger—a bourgeois who's gone wrong.'

He didn't say a word. Then he stood up resolutely and took up his hat and stick.

'I'm grateful, Lisaveta Ivanovna; now I can go home relieved. *Whoever I am has been settled and solved.*'

5

It was around autumn that Tonio Kröger said to Lisaveta Ivanovna:

'I'm off travelling now, Lisaveta: I need a breath of fresh air, I'm taking myself away, I'm going out into the wide world.'

'So what is it now, my dear German friend, are you keen to give Italy the privilege of a return visit?'

'Goodness, leave Italy out of it, Lisaveta! I'm so indifferent
to Italy, to the point of really not caring for it. It's long ago that
I imagined I belonged there. Art, isn't that what Italy's about? A
velvety blue sky, superb wine and sweet joy for the senses... To
put it briefly, I don't want any of that. I'm giving it up. *Bellezza*,
the whole scene of beauty upsets me. Also I can't stand all those
vigorous, vibrant people in that country, with their dark animally
gaze. Those Romans have no conscience in their eyes... No, I'm
going to Denmark for a bit.'

'To Denmark?'

'Yes. I'm looking forward to it. I think it will turn out well.
As it happens I've never been there, up north, even though I
spent my entire youth living on the border, and still I've always
known the place and loved it. I expect I get this desire to be
in the north from my father, for in fact my mother was rather
more one for the *bellezza*, insofar as she was not quite indifferent
to everything. But take the books written there, deep, unsullied,
humorous books, Lisaveta—I don't mind what anyone says, I
love them. Take their Scandinavian meals, those incomparable
meals that one can only cope with in vigorous sea air (I don't
know whether I'll be able to manage them any more), and which
I know a bit from home, for that's pretty much how we eat in
my family. Take just the names, the forenames, that adorn the
people up there and of which there are, by the same token, a
lot round our way, a name like 'Ingeborg', it's perfect poetry,
like the sound of a harp. And then the sea—they have the Baltic
up that way...! In a word, I'm going north, Lisaveta. I want to
see the Baltic Sea again, I want to hear these names again, and
I want to read these books close to home, where they belong;
another thing I want is to stand on the terrace at Kronborg,
where Hamlet saw the "ghost" and, poor noble young fellow, was

plunged into morbid strife... desperate, always thinking about death...'

'How will you be travelling, Tonio, may I ask? What route will you take?'

'The usual one,' he said, shrugging his shoulders and visibly blushing. 'Yes, I'll make contact with my—with the place where I set off from, thirteen years ago. I imagine it may be rather comic.'

She smiled.

'That's what I wanted to hear, Tonio Kröger. God be with you. Don't forget to write to me, do you hear? I want to hear about all your adventures. I'm looking forward to a very lively letter from your journey—to Denmark...'

6

So Tonio Kröger travelled north. He travelled first-class (for, as he used to say, someone like me who has so many more inner troubles than other people can legitimately claim a little outward comfort), and he didn't stop until the towers of the town he had left behind, with its narrow little streets, stood out again before his eyes against the grey sky. He paused his journey there for a short while, and it was strange...

An overcast afternoon was already turning to evening when the train pulled into the narrow, fuggy station that was so wonderfully familiar to him. Great clouds of smoke lingered under the dirty glass roof and dissipated in long, thin streaks, just as it had been then when Tonio Kröger, his heart incapable of anything but jeering, had taken himself off. He took care of his luggage, arranged to have it brought to his hotel, and walked out into the street.

Standing outside in a row were the black two-horse droshkies, unusually high and broad. He didn't take one; he just looked at them, as he looked at everything, the narrow gables and the pointed towers, to which he said hello over the roofs in front of him, and the blond, easy-going, not specially refined people with their broad, rapid way of speaking all around him, and he felt an anxious laughter rise inside him that had a secret affinity with sobbing. He went on foot, slowly, with the unremitting damp wind slapping him in the face, over the bridge with the mythological figures on the railings, and then he walked for a while beside the harbour.

Lord above, how tiny and cramped the whole place seemed! Had it been the case all along that these narrow alleys overhung with gables rose so dead straight up into the town? The chimneys and the ships' masts were gently swaying in the wind on the darkened river as evening fell. Should he go up that street, that one there, where the house stood that he was thinking about? No, tomorrow. He was sleepy now. His head weighed on him after the journey, and slow, foggy thoughts passed through his mind.

Now and again in these last thirteen years, when his stomach was complaining of the excesses of his life, he'd had a dream that he was once again at home in the old, echoing house on the steep lane, that his father was there again and giving him a good telling-off with regard to his depraved lifestyle, and each time he found that quite in order. And this present moment did not differ a whit from one of those maddening inescapable nightmares in which you have to ask yourself whether you're deceiving yourself or is this reality, and feel the compelling weight of a decision in favour of the latter, but then in the end you wake up… He walked through the draughty streets. There were few people about. He held his head bent against the wind and proceeded like a sleepwalker in the direction of the hotel, the best in town, where he was to spend the night. A man with bandy legs, carrying a pole on the top of which a little flame was burning, walked ahead of him, weaving his way like a sailor, and lit the gas lanterns.

How did he feel? What was it that, though it never became a proper fire, was glowing so darkly and painfully beneath the ashes of his tiredness? Quiet, quiet, not a word! Don't say anything! He would happily have walked on in the wind through the darkening alleys that appeared to him as if in a dream of home. But everything was so narrow and crammed together. He'd soon be there.

In the upper town there were lamps that arced over the street, and they were just coming on. There was the hotel, and there the two black lions he'd been afraid of as a child. They were just the same as they had always been, looking at each other as if they wanted to sneeze; but they seemed to have got much smaller. Tonio Kröger passed between them.

Since he arrived on foot no one made much fuss of him. The doorkeeper and a very slender gentleman dressed in black, who did the honours and with his little finger kept pushing his cuffs back into his sleeves, ran their eyes over him, weighing him up from head to toe, visibly trying to place him socially, to establish his place in the hierarchy, what part of the middle class he belonged to, and to allot him a place of due respect, without reaching a satisfactory conclusion, whereupon they decided on a modest degree of politeness. A waiter, an unobtrusive man with ash-blond sideburns, an evening jacket shiny with age and rosettes on his silent shoes, led him up two steps to a nice enough room. The décor was old-fashioned and it looked out in the twilight on to a picturesque, medieval view of courtyards, gables and the extraordinary heaviness of the church situated beside the hotel. Tonio Kröger stood in front of this window for a while; then he sat on the broad, comfortable sofa, crossed his arms, knitted his brows together and whistled a tune.

They came with a light, and his luggage arrived. At the same time the unobtrusive waiter put a slip of paper on the table that he needed to fill in to register his arrival, and Tonio, holding his head to one side, embellished it with something that looked like name, employment and place of origin. That done, he ordered a small cold supper, just bread and something to go with it, and continued from his corner of the sofa to stare into space. The food arrived but it was a long time before he touched it. He finally took a couple of bites and then spent an hour pacing up and down the room, stopping every now and again and closing his eyes. Then he undressed slowly, with careful movements, and went to bed. He slept a long time and had confused dreams full of the strangest longings.

When he woke up he saw that his room was filled with daylight. Hastily coming to his senses, he established where he was and went to open the curtains. The late-summer blue of the sky, already a little pale, was shot through with little patches of cloud whipped up by the wind; but the sun was shining over the town of his birth.

He took greater pains than usual with his morning toilette, washed and shaved to precision, and made himself neat and tidy, as if he were about to pay a visit to a very correct house of good standing where it mattered to make a polished and immaculate impression; and while he went through the motions of getting dressed he listened to the anxious pounding of his heart.

How light it was outside! He might have felt better had the streets been in near-darkness, like yesterday; now he had to appear in front of people in bright sunshine. Would he meet people he knew, who would stop and ask him something, and he would have to tell them how he had spent the last thirteen years? No, thank God, no one knew him any more, and anyone who remembered him wouldn't recognize him, for he really had changed quite a bit in between. He had a good look at himself in the mirror and suddenly he felt more secure behind the mask he had devised for himself early on, whereby he looked older than his years... He ordered breakfast and then he went out, under the critical eyes of the doorkeeper and the well-dressed man in black, through the vestibule, out between the lions and into the open air.

Where did he go? He scarcely knew. It was like yesterday. Hardly had he immersed himself in this wondrous, stately and deeply loved jumble of gables, turrets, arcades and fountains, hardly did he feel once again on his face the pressure of the wind, the strong wind that brought with it a delicate, bitter aroma of far-off dreams, than his senses became completely befuddled, dissolving in mists, caught up in webs of delusion... the muscles of his face relaxed; and with his now calm gaze he regarded the people and the things. Perhaps it was on that street corner that he woke up...

Where did he go? It seemed to him that the direction he set off in was connected to the sad dreams he'd had that night, so strange and full of regret. He went to the market, under the vaulted arcades beneath the town hall, where butchers with bloody hands were weighing their wares, walked through to the market square where the tall Gothic fountain stood with all its different pinnacles. There he came to a halt in front of one of the houses, narrow and simple, like the others with a curved, open gable, and lost himself in contemplation. He read the name on the door and let his eyes rest a while on each of the windows. Then he turned slowly and walked off.

Where did he go? Towards home. But he took a roundabout way, walked to the Gate, because he had time to spare. He went along the Mühlenwall and the Holstenwall and had to hang on to his hat in the wind, which moaned and groaned in the trees. Then he left the ramparts not far from the station, watched a train huff and puff its way along as it slowly picked up speed, amused himself counting the number of carriages and followed with his eyes the man sitting high up in the last one of all. But when he got to the Lindenplatz he stopped in front of one of the handsome villas that stood there, spent a long time surveying the garden and looking up to each of the windows, and finally got the idea to push the iron gate back and forth on its hinges and make it squeak. He spent some time looking at his hand, which had become cold and covered in rust, and went on, through the sturdy old entrance tower, along the harbour and up the steep, draughty alleyway to his parents' house.

It stood there, enclosed by the neighbouring houses that towered over its gable, grey and severe as it had been for the last three hundred years, and Tonio Kröger read the pious inscription that stood over the entrance, its letters half worn away. Then he sighed with relief and went inside.

His heart was beating anxiously, for he could quite imagine his father coming out of one of the doors on the ground floor and, standing there on the threshold, in his office jacket and with a quill pen behind his ear, buttonholing him and giving him a strong talking-to with regard to his extravagant life, and he would feel that was perfectly in order. But he walked up and no light appeared. The inner door that stopped the wind coming in was not locked, just pulled to, and he found that reprehensible, while at the same time he had the sense that one sometimes gets in happy dreams in which the obstacles just melt away of themselves and by some magic one makes one's way forwards without hindrance… His footsteps echoed along the broad corridor with its large flagstones. Opposite the kitchen, where all was quiet, he could see at some height the strange, crude but neatly varnished wooden storage rooms protruding from the wall as they had done for ages. These were the maids' rooms, which could only be reached by way of a free-standing staircase from the corridor. But the large cupboards that used to stand there were gone, as was the carved chest... The son of the house embarked upon the massive staircase and rested his hand on the white-painted open banister, lifting it and letting it fall gently with each step he took, as if he were trying cautiously to see if his old intimacy with this solid banister could be re-established... but then he stopped on the stairs, in front of the entrance to the mezzanine floor. Stuck on the door there was a sign in white saying, in black letters: Community Library.

Community Library? thought Tonio Kröger, reflecting that here was no place for community, neither for literature. He knocked on the door... Someone suggested he come in and so in he went. Tense and angry, his eyes greeted changes that seemed to him highly inappropriate.

The mezzanine floor was three rooms deep, and the doors connecting them stood open. The walls were covered almost right up to the top with identically bound books standing on dark shelves in long rows. In every room behind a table like a shop counter some nondescript fellow was sitting and writing. Two of them merely turned their heads in Tonio Kröger's direction, but the first one sprang to his feet, propping himself up with both hands on the surface of the desk, thrust his head forwards, pointed his lips, raised his eyebrows and, blinking rapidly, stared at the visitor...

'Forgive me,' said Tonio Kröger, without taking his eyes off the books. 'I'm a stranger here, I'm visiting the town. So this is the Community Library? Would you mind if I had a bit of a look at the collection?'

'With pleasure!' said the official, and blinked even faster... 'Of course. Anyone is free to do that. Do you want just to look around or would you like to avail yourself of the catalogue?'

'Thank you,' said Tonio Kröger, 'I can find my way around.' And so he began to make his way slowly around the walls, giving the impression that he was reading the titles on the spines. Finally he took out a volume, opened it and positioned himself with it at the window.

This is where they had the breakfast room. They used to have breakfast here in the mornings, rather than upstairs in the big dining room, where white statues of gods and goddesses stood out against the blue wallpaper... And that room over there had been a bedroom. His father's mother died there, very old, and suffered greatly on the way because she was a worldly woman who liked her pleasures and didn't want to go. And later his father too had breathed his last there, that tall, correct, faintly melancholy and thoughtful gentleman with the poppy in his buttonhole... Tonio had sat at the end of his deathbed with burning eyes, abandoning himself honestly and entirely to a strong, wordless emotion, to love and pain. Even his mother had knelt there, his beautiful, fiery mother, dissolved in hot tears; whereupon she moved with her artist from the south to a faraway place with a blue sky... But there right at the back, the smaller third room, now also full of books, supervised by some nondescript fellow, was the one that for many years had been his own. That was where he went when he came home from school, after he'd been for a walk, just as now, his desk had stood against that wall, and it was into its drawer that he had consigned his first heartfelt and hapless poems... The walnut tree... A terrible feeling of loss pierced him, and he trembled. He looked across and out of the window. The garden was overgrown and seemed abandoned, but the old walnut tree was still standing there, on its spot, groaning stiffly and rustling in the wind. And Tonio Kröger let his eyes drift back to the book he was holding, an outstanding work of literature that was well known to him. He looked down at the black lines and paragraphs, let himself be caught up in the sophisticated flow of the narrative for a while, followed how the writer found images to clothe some passionate feeling, such that he could bring his writing to a head, make his point and let it have its effect on the reader, before equally effectively moving on…

'Yes, that's well done,' he said, put the book away and turned. Then he noticed that the official was still on his feet and was blinking with a mixture of professional zeal and a mistrust that he'd been turning over in his mind.

'An excellent collection, as I see it,' said Tonio Kröger. 'I've got the general idea. I'm very grateful to you. Adieu.' And with that he went to the door; but it was a departure that left a certain dubiousness in its wake, and he could clearly foresee how the official, thoroughly troubled by this visit, would go on standing there for minutes after he'd gone, his eyes blinking.

He felt no inclination to press on further. He'd been home. On the upper floors, in the big rooms behind the hall of columns, strangers were living, he could see that; for they'd closed off the top of the stairs with a glass door that hadn't been there before, and there was a nameplate on it. He went on, down the staircase, along the echoing corridor, and left his parents' house. He went into a restaurant, took a corner table and sat, thoroughly turned in on himself, eating a heavy, fatty meal, and then he went back to the hotel.

'I've come to the end of my stay,' he said to the *soigné* gentleman in black. 'I'll be leaving this afternoon. And he asked for his bill and ordered a cab to take him to the harbour for the steamer to Copenhagen. Then he went up to his room and sat at the table, sat there upright and silent, with his cheeks in his hands and looking down at the tabletop with eyes that saw nothing. Later he settled his bill and readied his belongings. The cab was announced at the arranged time and Tonio Kröger went down the staircase, ready for his journey.

At the bottom the *soigné* gentleman in black was waiting for him. 'Excuse me,' he said, and with his little fingers pushed his cuffs back under his sleeves... 'Do forgive me, sir, for claiming just another moment of your time. Herr Seehaase—who owns the hotel—just wanted a few words. A formality. He's over there... If you would be so kind as to come with me... It's *only* Herr Seehaase, the owner of the hotel.'

And with an inviting gesture he led Tonio Kröger to the far end of the vestibule. There indeed Herr Seehaase was standing. Tonio Kröger knew him by sight as of old. He was small and fleshy with bandy legs. His nicely trimmed whiskers had turned white; but he still wore a generously cut dinner jacket and with it a velvet cap with green embroidery. Nor was he alone. Standing beside him, next to a small desktop fixed to the wall, stood, with a helmet on his head, a policeman. His gloved right hand was resting on a piece of paper with writing all over it lying in front of him on the desktop, and with his honest face, the face of a soldier, he was looking at Tonio Kröger as if he expected him to sink into the ground at the sight of him.

Tonio Kröger looked from one to the other and resigned himself to waiting.

'So you come from Munich?' asked the policeman finally, in his kindly and ponderous voice.

Tonio Kröger answered in the affirmative.

'And you're travelling to Copenhagen?'

'Yes, I'm on my way to a Danish seaside resort.'

'A seaside resort? Well you must produce your papers,' said the policeman, taking special satisfaction in the word 'produce'.

'Papers...' He had no papers. He took up his briefcase and looked inside; but apart from some money in notes there was nothing within but the proofs of a story that he had intended to work through on his journey. He didn't like dealing with officials and had never applied for a passport.

'I'm sorry,' he said, 'but I don't have any on me.'

'Is that the case?' said the policeman... 'None at all? What's your name?'

Tonio Kröger answered him.

'Can that be true?' asked the policeman, drawing himself up to his full height and suddenly flaring his nostrils as widely as he could...

'Entirely true,' replied Tonio Kröger.

'And what are you then?'

Tonio Kröger swallowed and in a firm voice named a trade. Herr Seehaase raised his head and looked up into his face with curiosity.

'Hm,' said the policeman. 'And you maintain that you are not one and the same as an iddivdal by the name of—' He said 'iddivdal' and then from the paper covered in writing spelt out a very complicated romantic name which seemed to be adventurously made up of sounds from various races and which Tonio Kröger promptly forgot again; '—an iddivdal,' he went on, 'of unknown parents and falling under some suspicion after a series of deceptions and other offences and now wanted by the Munich police and probably fleeing to Denmark?'

'I'm not just maintaining it. I'm saying I am not that person,' said Tonio Kröger, and shrugged his shoulders nervously. This made a certain impression.

'I see. Well of course!' said the policeman. 'But you're also maintaining you don't have any papers to show for yourself!'

Herr Seehaase stepped in soothingly as a mediator.

'This is all just a formality,' he said, 'nothing more! As you can imagine, the officer is only doing his duty. If you could just verify your identity somehow... isn't there some piece of paper...'

They all fell silent. Should he make an end of it, should he make himself known by revealing to Herr Seehaase that he was no confidence trickster under suspicion from the police, not born a gypsy in a green caravan, but was the son of Consul Kröger, of the Kröger family? No, he had no desire to do that. And anyway, was there not something right about these gentlemen whose function was to uphold the middle-class order of things? In a way he was entirely in agreement with them... He shrugged his shoulders and said nothing.

'So what have you got in there?' asked the policeman. 'There, in your *portefeuille*.' (He said it in a peculiar local way.)

'In here? Nothing. It's a proof.'

'A proof? What do you mean a proof? Let me see.'

And Tonio Kröger handed over his work. The policeman spread it out on the little folding desk and began to read. Herr Seehaase too came closer and joined in the reading. Tonio Kröger watched over their shoulders and noted the place they'd arrived at. It was a good passage, where he'd made his point and let it take effect. It was excellently done and he was contented with himself.

'Look here!' he said. 'Here's my name. I wrote this and now it's about to be published, do you see?'

'So that's enough,' said Herr Seehaase decisively, as he shuffled the pages together, folded them and gave them back. 'Surely that's enough, Petersen!' he repeated, surreptitiously closing his eyes and shaking his head as if to draw things to a close. 'We mustn't detain this gentleman any longer. The cab is waiting. Dear sir, I do beg your pardon for this little intrusion. The officer was only doing his duty, although I said to him at once that he was on the wrong track…'

Is that so, thought Tonio Kröger.

The policeman didn't seem to be wholly in agreement; the issue of 'the iddividal' and 'producing' one's papers still bothered him. But Herr Seehaase, repeatedly expressing his regret, led his guest back through the vestibule, accompanied him down past the pair of lions to the cab and, calling to him to take care, shut the cab door. And then the absurdly tall and broad droshky began its stumbling, creaking, noisy journey through the steep alleyways and down to the harbour…

This was Tonio Kröger's peculiar stay in the town where he was born.

7

Night fell, and the moon was already out, casting a diffuse silver glow, when Tonio Kröger's ship reached the open sea. He stood in the bows, huddled in his cloak from the wind, which grew stronger and stronger, and stared down into the dark comings and goings of the waves, which overrode each other, crashed into each other and parted in unexpected directions. The spume suddenly flared up…

He was basking in a mood of silent delight. He'd been a little dispirited that in his old home town they'd wanted to arrest him as a confidence trickster—although he would have found it perfectly in order, in a way. But then, once he was on board, he had, as he had sometimes done with his father, turned to watch the loading of the ship. The voices shouting this and that were a mixture of Danish and Plattdeutsch, as they lowered all sorts of sacks and crates down into the hold, and also thick barred cages containing a polar bear and a Bengal tiger; presumably they came from Hamburg and were destined for a Danish zoo; and all this he found very entertaining. Then, in the time it took the ship to glide between the flat banks of the river, he completely forgot about being questioned by the policeman Petersen and all that had happened before, his sad, sweet dreams at night, full of regrets, the walk that he took, the sight of the walnut tree, all that had once again a firm place in his heart. And now, as the sea broadened out, he saw from a distance the beach where as a boy he had had the happy chance to listen in on its summer dreams, saw the beam of the lighthouse and the lights of the spa hotel where he had stayed with his parents... The Baltic! He turned his head into the strong, salty wind that blew uninterruptedly and freely off it, wrapped itself around his ears and made him mildly dizzy and slightly numb, and in that state the memory of everything bad, the torment and confusion, everything he had wanted and all that had troubled him slowly vanished. Its power ebbed and he felt blissful. And in the rushing, slapping, foaming and groaning that filled his ears he thought he could hear the rustling and creaking of the old walnut tree and the squeaking of the garden gate... It got darker and darker.

'My godd, the zdars, just look at those zdars,' said a voice all of a sudden. It had a ponderous, sing-song intonation, pronounced the word 'star' peculiarly, and seemed to come from inside a barrel. He knew whose it was. It belonged to a simply dressed man, with pale-red hair, who looked cold and wet through, as if he'd just had a swim, and whose eyelids were red. He'd been Tonio Kröger's neighbour in the dining room when they ate their evening meal, and had had in all modesty cautiously helped himself to an astonishing quantity of lobster omelette. Now he was beside him leaning on the rail and looking up to the sky, his chin propped on his thumb and index finger. Undoubtedly, he found himself in the kind of extraordinary and exalted mood in which inhibitions between people fall away, when people open their hearts even to strangers, and things pass people's lips that they would normally be too shy to come out with...

'Just look, sir, at those zdars. There they stand and twinkle, Godd knows, the whole sky is full of them. And I ask you, when a fellow looks up at them and considers that many of them are said to be a hundred times bigger than the Earth, what's he supposed to make of that? We humans have invented the telegraph and the telephone and so many achievements of modern times, by Jove we have. But when we look up there, we have to accept and understand that basically we're just a pack of worms, a miserable pack of worms and nothing more—am I right or not, my dear sir? Yes, we're a pack of worms!' he answered himself and nodded, respectful and contrite, in the direction of the firmament.

Oh yo yo, this chap's got no literature in him! thought Tonio Kröger. And just then he remembered something he had read recently, an essay by a famous French writer about cosmology and psychology; he'd made a pretty good job of it.

He gave the young man something by way of a response to the experience that had struck him so deeply, and then they continued to talk, still leaning over the rail and staring out into the disturbingly lit, eventful evening. It turned out that his travelling companion was a young businessman from Hamburg who was using his leave to take this trip for pleasure...

'Told myself I should give the zdeamer to Copenhagen a go, and so here I am and so far it's pretty good. I didn't get it right with the lobster omelette though, you'll see that, sir, it's going to be rough tonight, the cap'n said it himself, and to have indigestible food like that in your belly will be no fun...'

Tonio Kröger listened with friendly feelings to all this familiar nonsense. He felt at home.

'Yes,' he said, ' the food here up north is altogether too heavy. It can make you feel indolent and rather melancholy.'

'Melancholy?' repeated the young man, and looked at him perplexed... 'You're a stranger here, sir, I suppose?' he asked suddenly...

'That's right, yes, I come from far away!' replied Tonio Kröger, with a vague gesture into the blue.

'But you're right,' said the young man; 'damn it all you're absolutely right in what you say about melancholy! I'm almost always melancholy, but particularly on evenings like this, when the zdars are out in the sky.' And he rested his chin on his thumb and index finger again.

I'm sure he writes poetry, thought Tonio Kröger, deeply felt, sincere businessman's poems...

The evening moved on, and the wind was now so strong it made it difficult to speak. So they decided to get some sleep, and wished each other a good night.

Tonio Kröger stretched out in his cabin on the narrow bunk, but he couldn't settle. The strong wind and its bitter scent had strangely upset him, and his heart was pounding as if he were waiting for something sweetly pleasurable to happen. It was a shock too, and made him feel terribly ill when the ship came down the other side of a tall wave and the propeller was stuck working in mid-air. He got fully dressed again and went outside.

Clouds raced past the moon. The sea danced. The waves didn't flow in order, evenly and roundly, but converged from far off; everywhere he could see in the pale and flickering light the sea was being torn apart; it was whipped up and agitated; it licked up and leapt high in gigantic pointed tongues like flames, creating jagged, unreal scenes against the background of great foaming cliffs and then hurling the spray in every direction, as if monstrous arms were playing a mad game to test their strength. The ship was having a difficult passage; pounding and swaying and groaning as it struggled through the tumult, and now and again one could hear the polar bear and the tiger, suffering from seasickness, bellow from the hold. A man in oilskins, with a sou'wester on his head and a lantern fastened round his chest, was moving about the foredeck, his legs spaced wide apart as he tried to balance. But there right at the back stood the young man from Hamburg and he was having a bad time of it. 'My Godd,' he said with a hollow, unsteady voice, as he caught sight of Tonio Kröger, 'just look at that for a clash of the elements, my dear sir!' But then he was interrupted and quickly turned away.

Tonio Kröger held on to a taut rope and gazed out at the fierce, unruly scene. A triumphant cry of joy welled up in him, and it seemed loud enough to outdo all that the storm and the sea had to offer. A hymn to the sea, a hymn full of love, sounded in his head. My friend so wild of younger days / again we find ourselves as one... But then the poem was over. It was not polished, it didn't have the right shape and was never to be worked up in tranquillity into a greater whole. His heart was alive...

He stood there for a long time; then he stretched himself out on a bench outside the dining room and looked up at the sky where the stars twinkled. He even half fell asleep. And when the cold spray splashed in his face it was like pillow talk in slumber.

Vertical chalk cliffs, ghostly in the moonlight, came into view and grew nearer; it was the island of Møn. And once again sleep intervened, interrupted by showers of salty spume that bit sharply into his face and froze his features... When he was fully awake it was already day, a fresh, light-grey day, and the green sea had calmed down. At breakfast he saw the young businessman again and the latter blushed furiously, probably ashamed to have come out with those embarrassing poetic sentiments in the dark. He pushed up his reddish little moustache with all five fingers and in soldierly fashion wished him a crisp good morning, only then to set about avoiding him.

And Tonio Kröger landed in Denmark. He arrived in Copenhagen, gave a tip to everyone who looked as if they deserved it, and then, from his hotel room, spent three days wandering about the city, carrying his guidebook in front of him, and behaved just like the better kind of traveller who wanted to enlarge his knowledge. He looked at the King's New Square and the 'horse' in the middle, paid his respects by staring up at the columns of the Church of Our Lady, stood for a long time in front of Thorvaldsen's noble and charming sculptures, climbed up the round tower, visited castles and spent two jolly evenings in the Tivoli Gardens. But this wasn't exactly what he saw.

On the houses that often resembled the old houses in his native town, with their rounded, open gables, he saw names that were familiar to him from the old days that seemed to signify something gentle and delightful and withal to contain an element of reproach, lament and a longing for what was lost. And everywhere, as in slow, thoughtful draughts he breathed in the damp sea air, he saw eyes that were so blue, hair that was so blond, faces that were of a shape and form such as he had seen in his peculiarly painful dreams, full of remorse, that had come to him during the night he spent in his home town. It sometimes happened that in the middle of the street a look, a word out loud, a burst of laughter could pierce him to the core...

He couldn't bear to stay long in the lively city. Unrest gripped him, all sweetness and folly, half memory and half expectation, together with the desire to be able to lie quietly on the beach somewhere and not to have to play the role of the busy tourist seeing the sights. So he boarded another ship and on a dull day (the sea looked black) travelled north along the Seeland coast towards Helsingør. From there he immediately transferred to a cab that made its way along the main road for another three-quarters of an hour, always just above the sea, until he reached his final and actual destination, the little white hotel on the water with the green shutters that stood in the middle of a group of small, low houses and with its wooden-clad tower looked out on the sound and the Swedish coast. Here he got out and took possession of the light-filled room that had been reserved for him. There was a little shelf in the room, and a locker, and there he stowed the things he had with him and set himself to stay here for a while.

8

It was now almost September; not many guests remained in Ålsgårde. At meals in the large dining room with exposed beams on the ground floor, whose tall windows looked out on to the glassed-in solarium and the sea, it was the hotel owner who waited at table. She was getting on in years, a spinster with white hair, colourless eyes, pink cheeks and an impossible twittering voice. She kept trying to find a way of presenting her red hands so that they looked a little better on the white tablecloth. An old man with a short neck, an ice-grey mutton-chop moustache and a face with a dark-blue look, was there, a fishmonger from the capital who knew German. He gave the impression of being thoroughly constipated and inclined to apoplexy, for his breath was short and came out in bursts and every now and again he lifted his beringed index finger to one of his nostrils to close it and to get some air into the other one by blowing out hard through it. That didn't stop him keeping up a continuous conversation with the aquavit bottle which stood on his table at breakfast too, as well as at lunch and dinner. Otherwise there were just three tall American youths with their tutor or *gouverneur*, who silently fiddled with his spectacles and played football with them during the day. They wore their reddish-blond hair with a parting in the middle and had long, impassive faces. 'Please, pass me that wurst or whatever it is!' said the one. 'That's not wurst; that's *Schinken*!' said the other (for cured meats are not the same as ham). And this was all that came out of them, and also from the tutor, by way of conversation; otherwise they just sat there in silence and drank hot water.

Tonio Kröger couldn't have wished for better dining companions. He enjoyed his peace, cast an ear in the direction of the particular sound Danish makes in the throat, and the bright and occluded vowels which featured in occasional exchanges between the fishmonger and the hotel owner, exchanged from time to time with the former some simple observation about the state of the barometer, then stood up and took himself off by way of the solarium and back down to the beach, where he had been spending the long hours of the morning.

Sometimes it was quiet and like summer. The sea was calm and smooth, striped blue, bottle-green and red, with a glittering sliver light playing over the surface, the seaweed became golden and turned to hay in the sun, and the jellyfish lay there and dried out. It smelt a bit rotten and a bit too of the tar that belonged to the fishing boat against which Tonio Kröger, sitting on the sand, was leaning his back—he was turned so that he had the open sea and not the Swedish coastline before his eyes; but the gentle breeze from the sea left everything it touched fresh and clean in its wake.

Then grey, stormy days arrived. The waves lowered their heads like bulls pointing their horns and about to charge, and smashed angrily against the beach, where the tide ran high and left it covered with gleaming wet seagrass, shells and driftwood. Between the crests of the broad, sweeping waves stretched out, under the overcast sky, the troughs, pale green and foaming; but where the sun was behind the clouds a whiteish velvet sheen lay on the water.

Tonio stood wrapped up against the raging wind, steeped in this eternal, oppressive, numbing fury that he loved so much. If he turned and went away, it suddenly struck him as quite calm and warm all around him. But then he was aware of the sea behind him; it called to him, tempted him, shouted out a greeting. And he smiled.

He took a path inland, across the meadows, through solitary places, and very soon a beech wood enclosed him, which reached uphill and far into the distance. He sat down on some moss, leaning on a tree, so that he could see between the branches a strip of the sea. Now and again the wind brought the sound of the surf right close to him, it sounded like boards collapsing one after another far away. Crows shrieked in the treetops, hoarse, bleak and abandoned... He kept his book on his knee but read not a word of it. He enjoyed a deep forgetting, a hovering outside of space and time that redeemed him, and only now and again was it that his heart trembled at some sadness, a brief stab of longing or regret, whose name and origin he was too lazy and otherwise absorbed to ask after.

Many a day passed like that; he couldn't have said how many and had no desire to find out how long he had been there. But then came an hour in which something happened; it happened when the sun was in the sky and people were around, and Tonio Kröger was not particularly surprised that it did.

There was something grand and enchanting about that day from the beginning. Tonio Kröger woke very early and suddenly. He opened his eyes and sat up as if in some vague shock he couldn't put his finger on, and believed, as if in a miracle, to be gazing on a magically lit fairy tale. His room, with its glass door and balcony facing out towards the sound, and separated from the main bedroom and living area by a thin white gauze curtain, was papered with a delicate pattern on the walls and filled with pale, light furniture, so that it constantly gave off a friendly and inviting look. And now his eyes, still full of sleep, saw it undergo an unearthly transformation and illumination, bathed over and over in an inexpressibly beautiful and fragrant pink glow, which turned the walls and the furniture golden and suffused the gauze curtain in a soft red gleam... Tonio Kröger took a long time before he realized what was happening. But then, when he went and stood in front of the glass door and looked out, he saw that the sun was rising.

For several days it had been dull and rainy; but now the sky stretched out like taut pale-blue silk dazzlingly clear over sea and land, and, criss-crossed and surrounded by clouds suffused in red and gold, the first sign of the sun rose majestically above the shimmering, choppy sea, which seemed to shudder and burst into flame... So the day began to take its course, and Tonio happily threw on his clothes, was the first down to breakfast in the solarium, and thereupon from the little wooden beach hut swam a distance out into the sound, then walked for an hour along the beach. When he came back there were a number of omnibus-like vehicles parked outside the hotel and from the dining room he could see that in the neighbouring lounge, where the piano stood, as well as in the solarium and out on the terrace, a large number of people, dressed in lower-middle-class fashion, were sitting at round tables and, while enjoying excited conversations, drinking beer and eating sandwiches. There were whole families, older and young people, and even a couple of children.

As he enjoyed a second breakfast (the hotel offered a generous cold table, with smoked meats, salted dishes and baked goods), he asked what was happening.

'Guests!' said the fishmonger. 'Day-trippers from Helsingør and people who've come for the dance! God forbid we won't be able to sleep tonight! There's going to be a ball, with dancing and music, and it is to be feared it will go on late. It's a family get-together, a country outing and a reunion wrapped up in one, some kind of trip they've paid for, and they're enjoying the beautiful weather. They arrived in boats and by road, and now they're having breakfast. Later there's an excursion into the countryside, then they come back and then there's dancing and fun and games here in the dining room. Damn and blast it, we'll never sleep a wink...'

'Looks like fun,' said Tonio Kröger.

Whereupon nothing more was said for a while. The hotel owner tried to make the best of her red fingers, the fishmonger blew through his right nostril to unblock it, and the Americans drank hot water and pulled long faces as they did so.

Then what happened was this: *Hans Hansen and Ingeborg Holm crossed the room.*

Tonio Kröger, feeling pleasantly tired after his swim and energetic walk, was leaning back in his chair and eating smoked salmon on toast; he sat turned towards the solarium and the sea. And suddenly the door opened and the two came in hand in hand—taking their time, not rushing. Ingeborg, blonde Inge, was dressed in pale colours, the way she was for Herr Knaak's dance class. Her light, flowery dress reached only to her ankles, and round her shoulders she wore a loose white tulle bolero, which was sharply cut away to reveal her velvety-soft throat. Her hat, its ribbons tied together, hung over her arm. She was perhaps a little more grown up than before and now wore her wonderful thick hair wound round her head; but Hans Hansen was just as he had always been. He was wearing his sailor's reefer jacket with the gold buttons and the wide blue collar covering it on his shoulders and back; his seaman's cap with the short ribbons he held in the hand hanging down beside him and waved it to and fro. Ingeborg kept her narrow, almond-shaped gaze averted, as if she were a bit shy of being watched by the people eating. Only Hans Hansen turned his head directly to the breakfast table and, the world be damned, examined the people one after the other with his steel-blue eyes, full of expectation and a bit contemptuous; he let go of Ingeborg's hand and put ever more energy into swinging his hat back and forth, to show what a man he was. Like that they walked past Tonio, with the calm blue sea in the background, took in the length of the room and disappeared through the door at the opposite end into the piano room.

All this took place at eleven-thirty in the morning, and while the hotel guests were still at breakfast, the company next door and in the solarium got up and left the hotel by a side door they discovered, with no one setting foot in the dining room. They could be heard getting into their vehicles, joking and laughing, and then one after another sets of wheels began rolling and with a crunch they set off along the main road...

'You say they're coming back?' asked Tonio Kröger...

'Indeed!' said the fishmonger. 'Heaven forbid! They've ordered music and, let me tell you, my bedroom is up here, above the dining room.'

'It looks like fun,' Tonio Kröger repeated. Then he stood up and left.

He spent the day, as he had spent the others, on the beach, in the woods, held a book on his knee and blinked out into the sun. He toyed with a single idea: that they would be coming back and enjoying a dance in the dining room, as the fishmonger had promised; and he did nothing but look forward to it, with such a sweet, anxious joy as he had not experienced all through the dead years. Once, as one idea led to another, he fleetingly remembered someone he vaguely knew, the novelist Adelbert, who knew what he wanted, and went into the coffee house to escape the fresh air of spring. Thinking of him he shrugged...

Lunch was taken earlier than usual, and in the evening too they sat down sooner than usual, in the piano room, because the dining room was already being set up for the dance; the elaborate preparations upset everything. Then, when it was already dark and Tonio Kröger was sitting in his room, there was some activity again out on the main road and in the building. The excursionists had returned; what was more, still more guests were arriving from the direction of Helsingør, by various means of transport, and soon there could be heard from below the sound of a fiddle tuning up, and a clarinet playing its nasal scales...

Everything promised a gala evening of dancing ahead.

Now the little orchestra struck up a march; modestly and in strict tempo the sound drifted upstairs; they began the dance with a polonaise. Tonio Kröger sat still and listened for a while. But once he heard the march give way to a waltz, he got up and glided from his room without a sound.

From the corridor where his room lay you could take a back staircase to the side entrance of the hotel and from there reach the solarium without entering another room. This is the route he took, softly and furtively, as if he had chosen a forbidden path, and felt his way cautiously through the dark, irrepressibly attracted by this silly music that was balm to his soul—music whose bold, forthright tones were now ringing out and filling his ears.

The solarium was empty and the lights were off, but the glass door to the dining room, where two large petroleum lamps with polished reflectors were blazing bright, stood open. He crept over in that direction, treading softly, and the stolen joy of being able to stand here in the dark and watch those who were dancing in the light made his skin prickle. He was like a thief. Hastily and hungrily he sent out his eyes to search for the pair he wanted to see…

The party seemed well under way even though it had hardly been going for half an hour. People were enjoying themselves freely; but then they'd arrived back already warm and excited in each other's company, after a whole day together, happy and without a care in the world. In the piano room, which Tonio Kröger could take in if he moved just a bit further forwards, a number of older gentlemen had gathered, smoking, drinking and playing cards; but others sat next to their wives in red plush chairs just inside the next room, beside the wall, and watched the dancing. They rested their hands on their parted knees and puffed out their cheeks to signal they were doing well in life, while the mothers, with their little bonnets on their heads and their hands together beneath their breasts, with their heads to one side, followed the antics of the young people. They had erected a stage on the long side of the room and that's where the musicians were giving their all. There was even a trumpet, blowing with a certain hesitation, taking care, as if it were afraid of its own voice, which nevertheless persisted and sounded out loudest of all… The dancing couples wove in and out and circled each other, while others walked about the room arm in arm. They weren't dressed for a ball, more like for a Sunday in summer spent outdoors; the men were in suits of a provincial cut, which one could see were not worn during the week to keep them at their best, and the young women were in light, pastel-coloured frocks with posies of wild flowers in their bodices. There were also a couple of children in the room who had their own way of dancing together, even when the musicians took a break. A lanky man in a nice little jacket the shape of a swallow's tail, a pretentious provincial who liked to please the ladies, with permed hair and a monocle, an assistant to someone high up in the post office or something like that, all in all like a comic figure out of a Danish novel made flesh, appeared to be the organizer of the party and master of ceremonies. Quick on his feet, perspiring and steeped in the occasion, he managed to be everywhere at once, gliding fussily through the room, contriving to launch himself on tiptoes. Those feet, on which he wore little flat, pointed military half-boots, he had a tricky way of crossing over each other while he swung his arms into the air. He arranged the groups of dancers, called for music, clapped his hands; all the while the ribbons from the big coloured bow he had fixed on his shoulder, as a mark of his importance, flew about. Now and again he turned his head lovingly towards the bow as it streamed out behind him.

They were both there, indeed, the couple who had glided past Tonio Kröger in the sunlight, he caught sight of them again and shuddered with joy as he homed in on them both almost simultaneously. Hans Hansen was standing really close to him, right by the door; standing with his legs apart and leaning a little forwards, he was fully focused on devouring a large piece of pound cake, holding his cupped hand to his chin to catch any crumbs. And over there against the wall sat Ingeborg Holm, blonde Inge, and in just that moment the man from the post office sashayed up to her, bowing elaborately, with one hand against his back and the other charmingly pressed against his chest, to ask her for the next

75

dance; but she shook her head and indicated that she needed to get her breath back and rest a while, whereupon the assistant post-office official sat down beside her.

Tonio watched those two, Hans and Ingeborg, who had caused him his earliest pains in love. They were Hans and Ingeborg not so much because of their distinguishing features and similarity of dress, but rather because they were examples of a human type, particular variants of the human race, a pale, blue-eyed and blond-haired kind that invoked an idea of bright innocence and good cheer at the same time as they were proud and self-contained, simple and somehow untouchable... He watched them, watched as Hans Hansen, just as he was then, always with a spring in his step, a well-built man, broad in the shoulders and narrow in the hips, stood there in his sailor suit, watched as Ingeborg, carried away by laughter, tipped her head to one side in a particular way, just as she had a particular way of putting her hand to the back of her head and making her thin sleeves ride up above her elbows. It was a little girl's hand, not particularly slender, not what you would call fine—and he was suddenly so overcome with such painful homesickness in his heart that he couldn't help disappearing back into the darkness so that no one could see his tortured face.

Had I forgotten you? he asked. No, never! Not you, Hans, nor you, dear blonde Inge! It was for you after all that I worked, and when my work was applauded, I took a secret look around to see if you were part of the audience... So have you read *Don Carlos* now, Hans Hansen, as you promised me when we were standing at your garden gate? Don't bother! I don't expect it of you any more. How can a king who weeps because he's lonely be your business? You shouldn't dim the shine in your eyes, you shouldn't make them dull with too much burrowing in poetry books and steeping yourself in melancholy... How wonderful it would be

76

to be like you! To start again, to grow up like you, to be decent, cheerful and simple, conventional, respectable and at one with God and the world. How wonderful to be loved by harmless, happy people, and to take you, Ingeborg Holm, for my wife, and have a son like you, Hans Hansen—free from the curse of deep knowledge and creative torment, to live, love and give thanks for a blessedly ordinary life...! To start again? But it wouldn't help. It would go the same way again—everything would happen again now as it happened then. For some people necessarily take the wrong path because no right way exists for them.

The music had stopped; it was the interval, and refreshments were being handed round. The assistant to someone high up in the post office went about in person with a tray of herring salad and served the ladies; but when he came to Ingeborg Holm he even went down on one knee, and she blushed with joy.

In the dining room people became aware of someone watching them from the glass door, and he found strange and curious looks coming his way out of the midst of handsome, overheated faces; but he didn't move. Ingeborg and Hans cast him a glance too, almost at the same time, with that complete indifference that can look like contempt. All of a sudden, though, he realized someone had spotted him and refused to take their eyes off him... he turned his head and immediately met that gaze he had felt penetrating him from across the room. A girl stood not far away from him, with a pale, narrow, fine face. He'd noticed her earlier. She hadn't danced a lot, she had not been specially sought after by the gentlemen, and he'd observed her sitting alone against the wall with her lips tightly closed. She was standing alone now too. She was wearing the same light, fragrant clothes as the others, but beneath the diaphanous material of her dress her bare shoulders loomed bony and meagre, and her scrawny neck looked so hollow between those pathetic shoulders that it seemed as if the silent girl was in some way deformed. Her hands, which were wearing thin half-gloves, she kept folded on her flat chest, in such a way that the fingers were just touching. With her head lowered, she looked up at Tonio Kröger with tearful black eyes. He turned away…

Here, very close to him, sat Hans and Ingeborg. He'd taken a seat next to her, perhaps she was his sister, and, surrounded by other red-faced specimens of the human race, they were eating and drinking, chatting and having a good time, calling out to each other volubly, teasing and fooling about and roaring with laughter. Could Tonio not get a little closer? Could he not address some light-hearted remark to him or her, whatever occurred to him, and which would at least make them respond with a smile? It would make him happy, he longed for that; he might then return to his room contented, in the knowledge that he had established some little contact with them. He reflected what he might say; but he didn't find the courage to come out with it. And of course it was the same as it always had been: they wouldn't understand him, would be rather alienated by what they heard, whatever he came up with. For their language was not his language.

Now the dance seemed to get going again. The assistant to someone high up in the post office sprang into action on diverse fronts. He rushed about encouraging people back on to the dance floor, moved the chairs and glasses out of their way with the help of the waiters, gave instructions to the musicians, and with a prod propelled in front of him one or two ditherers who didn't know where they were going. What was the plan? Groups of four pairs were forming squares… an awful memory made Tonio Kröger blush. They were dancing the quadrille.

The music struck up and the pairs bowed and stepped through each other. The swallow-tailed assistant took charge; he called out the next move in French, by God, and his pronunciation of the nasal 'n' was incomparably distinguished. Ingeborg Holm was dancing close by Tonio Kröger, in the group right beside the door. She moved in front of him, here and there, back and forth, stepping and turning; now and again he could smell the perfume of her hair, or was it from the delicate material of her dress, and when it happened he closed his eyes with a feeling familiar to him from long ago, whose bitter charm wafting his way he had been vaguely scenting all these last few days, and which now once again filled him with its sweet urgency. So what was it? Longing? Tenderness? Envy, Self-hatred?... *Moulinet des dames!* Were you laughing, dear blonde Inge, were you laughing at me when I danced the moulinet and made such a pitiful fool of myself? And would you laugh at me today just the same, when knowing I have become something like a famous man in the meantime? Yes you would, and you would be quite right! Even if, single-handedly, I had created the nine symphonies, *The World as Will and Idea*, and *The Last Judgement*—you would be entirely and eternally right to laugh... He looked at her, and remembered a line of poetry that hadn't occurred to him for a long time, yet which he had always kept in his heart and cherished: 'I want to sleep, but you must dance.' He knew so well the Nordic-melancholic outlook those words enshrined, the deep sincerity and the pathetically clumsy attitude to the world that spoke there. Sleep—to want to sleep, to long to live simply and in accordance with feelings that don't drive a person to seek the deed and the dance, but just let them live, with a sweet lack of ambition, and then still to have to dance, to be forced to turn all his mind to fulfilling the vast demands of Art, a dance indeed but which is like a knife dance. Tonio Kröger could never forget the humbling paradox that he had to dance because he was in love...

All of a sudden the atmosphere on the dance floor became both more animated and more relaxed. The squares had dispersed, and people were leaping and gliding everywhere; for after the quadrille came the galop. The couples flew past Tonio Kröger, chasséing, dashing forwards, overtaking each other, laughing briefly without even taking a breath, as the music just raced along. One girl emerged, caught up in the general surge, whizzing and spinning along. She had a fine, pale face and thin shoulders she carried too high. And suddenly, in front of him, people were stumbling, slipping and falling... The pale girl went down. She fell so heavily and so hard that it seemed almost dangerous, and her partner fell with her. The latter must have hurt himself so badly that he completely forgot his lady, then, still not back on his feet, he began, grimacing, to massage his knee with his hands; and the girl, apparently dazed by the fall, was still lying on the floor. Tonio Kröger stepped forwards, took hold of her gently under her arms and lifted her up. Tired out, confused and full of her misfortune, she looked up at him and suddenly her vulnerable face flushed a matt pink.

'Tak! O, mange tak!' she said, thanking him in Danish. Her dark eyes were tearful when she raised her head.

'You'd better not dance any more, Fräulein,' he said kindly. Then his eyes turned once more to find *them*, Hans and Inge, and moved away. He took his leave of the solarium and the ball and went up to his room.

He was carried away by the party in which he had not taken part, and tired because he was envious. It was just like it had been much earlier in his life. Just the same! With his face blazing he'd found a dark place to stand, full of pain at the sight of the blond ones, the lively ones, the happy ones—yes, at the sight of *you*— and had then disappeared. Someone must come soon! Ingeborg must come soon, she'd surely notice that he'd left, she'd want to steal after him, put a hand on his shoulder and say: 'Come back inside with us! Be happy! I love you…'. But she absolutely didn't come. Nothing of the kind happened. Yes, it was just like it used to be, and he was happy as he was then. For his heart was alive. So what had been happening all the meanwhile, in which he had become what he was now? Ossification; desolation; ice; and the life of the mind! And Art…!

He undressed, got into bed and turned out the light. He whispered two names into the pillow, that little concoction of Nordic syllables that seemed to him so pure, so unsullied, and which for him represented his original, authentic feelings of love, pain and happiness, represented Life, and honest, straightforward emotion, represented Home. He looked back at the years since then and right up to this day. He contemplated the sensual desert he had passed through, the adventures of the body that had consumed his nerves, adventures of thought too, which saw him eaten up by irony and knowingness, saw him hollowed out and crippled because he knew too much, worn down to half the man he was by the fevers and frosts of trying to achieve something creative, thrown, amid fits of conscience and with no ground beneath his feet, between crass extremes, saintliness here, sordidness there, hurled back and forth between them, sophisticated, impoverished, exhausted by cold, artificial, esoteric exaltations, utterly on the wrong path, devastated, desolate and sick—and he wept with remorse and a longing for Home.

It was dark and quiet all around him. But he could still hear the sound of Life reaching him dimly and soothingly from downstairs, Life in all its sweet and trivial three-quarter time. Life as a lovely tune with three beats in the bar.

9

Tonio Kröger sat in the north and wrote to his friend Lisaveta Ivanovna, as he had promised.

Dear Lisaveta down there in Arcadia, where I will soon be returning, he wrote. So here is something that might be called a letter, though it will surely disappoint you, for I'm minded to keep it fairly general. Not that I have nothing to tell, or that I have not experienced this and that after my fashion. When I was back home in my native town they even wanted to arrest me... but I'll tell you about that when I see you. I have days, at the moment, when I prefer, respecting all the craft of good writing, to say something general rather than tell stories.

Do you still remember, Lisaveta, how you once called me a bourgeois, a good citizen, you meant, but on the wrong path? You delivered your verdict at a moment when, distracted by other confessions that I'd allowed to escape from me, I admitted to you my love for what I call Life; and I wonder whether you knew how finely you had hit upon the truth, my love of the conventions, of everything that is ordinary, and my love of Life being one and the same. Travelling has given me a chance to think about it...

Let me tell you that my father was temperamentally a man from the north: thoughtful, thorough, correct because of a streak of puritanism and inclined to be melancholy; my mother, from an exotic background it was difficult to pin down, was beautiful, sensual, naïve, careless and passionate all at the same time, impulsive and dissolute. Beyond any doubt this was a combination that contained in itself both extraordinary possibilities and extraordinary dangers. What came out of it was this: a conventional man who lost his way in art, a bohemian always longing for the good behaviour he was brought up in, an artist with a bad conscience.

For it's my conventional conscience that persuades me to see in all the business of being an artist, all exceptionalism and all genius something deeply ambivalent, deeply disreputable, extremely dubious. That same conscience fills me with this terrible weakness for all that is simple, sincere and pleasantly normal, everything decent and nothing to do with matters of the mind, because I love it so much.

I have a foot in two worlds, I'm not at home in either of them, and therefore things are a bit difficult for me. You artists call me a conventional man, and they, the conventional ones, are tempted to arrest me... I don't know which offends me more. The conventional folk are stupid; you lovers of beauty, however, who call me phlegmatic and think I have no passion, should reflect that there is an art so profound that it finds no greater desire, finds nothing sweeter and more worthy of the human heart, than the bliss of ordinariness. It goes back to the beginning of time and answers to the fate of humanity.

I admire those proud, cold artists who venture forth in search of grand, demonic beauty and despise mere mortals—but I don't envy them. For if anything can turn a writer into a poet, it is my conventional man's love for the way ordinary human beings enjoy their lives. Everything by way of warmth, kindness and humour has its origin there, and it almost seems to me that it is that love the good book has in mind when it writes that a man may speak with the tongues of men and of angels, but if he have not love he is become no more than sounding brass or a clanging cymbal.

What I have done, Lisaveta, is nothing, not much, as good as nothing. I will manage something better, Lisaveta—that's a promise. As I'm writing I can hear the rushing of the sea close beside me and I close my eyes. I look into a world not yet born, just an outline of something that asks to be given order and form;

I see in a bustle of shadows human figures calling out to me that I should exorcize and redeem them; tragic figures, absurd figures, and those who are both at the same time—and I am very much on their side. But my deepest, and most deeply hidden love belongs to the blond, blue-eyed types, the ones who openly relish life, those people who are conventional, lovable and happy.

Don't hold this love against me, Lisaveta; it is good and productive. Longing dwells there and sadness and envy; a tiny bit of contempt; and a feeling of pure bliss.

(1903)

DISORDER AND
EARLY SORROW

THERE ARE ONLY vegetables for the main course—cabbage cutlets—so there is a pudding to follow, made with a powder tasting of almonds and soap, what the shops sell these days, and while Xaver, the youthful manservant, wearing a striped jacket that he has outgrown, gloves of white wool and yellow sandals, is serving it, the Grown-Ups, minded to spare him the worst, remind their father that they are expecting company that day.

The Grown-Ups are the eighteen-year-old, brown-eyed Ingrid, a very charming girl, who is just about to take her *Abitur*, and will probably pass it, if only because she has completely turned the heads of the teachers and in particular the headmaster, she not thinking actually to use her paper qualification, rather, on the basis of her agreeable smile, her gratifying voice and an exceptional and highly amusing gift for parody, to get into the theatre—and Bert, blond and seventeen, who has absolutely no desire to prolong his schooldays and wishes to throw himself into life as soon as possible and wants to become either a dancer or cabaret compère or, for the record, a waiter: this role to be taken up at 'The Cairo'—a destination to which at five in the morning he has already once tried and failed to run away and find refuge. He shows a definite similarity to Xaver Kleinsgütl, the servant, who is the same age; not because anyone could say he looks ordinary—in his features, indeed, he looks strikingly like his father, Professor Cornelius—but rather by virtue of an affinity in another direction, on the strength of a mutual coincidence of type, that at least, an overlap in which their similar clothes and general attitude play the chief role. Both wear the thick hair on their heads very long, fleetingly parted in the middle, and use the same movement of the head to flick it away from their brow as a result. Whenever one of them leaves the house by the garden gate and sets off on foot or gets on a bicycle—so then Doctor Cornelius, from the window of his bedroom, makes every effort to discern who it is. But then try as he might he can't decide who he has before him, the rough village lad or his own son. Bare-headed in any weather, in a windcheater fastened with a leather belt for no other reason but to look attractive, and with his upper body slightly bent forwards, his head inclined on his shoulder, who is that young man? Xaver, if he felt like it, would help himself to any of the family bicycles, men's or women's and even, in a particularly heedless mood, to the professor's own. Doctor Cornelius finds that the two lads both look like young *muzhiks*—Russian peasants—the one as much as the other. Further, both are passionate smokers, even if Bert doesn't have the means to smoke as many as Xaver, who on occasion sees off thirty in a day. He buys a brand bearing the name of a cinema goddess standing amid garlands.

The Grown-Ups call their parents the Old Folk—not behind their backs but directly, ever so fondly, to their faces, even though Cornelius is only forty-seven and his wife eight years younger still. 'Esteemed old chap!' they say. 'Faithful old girl!', on top of which, because of that way of talking, the professor's parents, who in his house lead the vaguely confused and closeted life of old people, get called the Prehistoric Folk. As for the Little Ones, Lorchen and Beißer, who eat their meal upstairs with 'Blue Anna'—named after her blue cheeks—they talk to their father the same way their mother does: they say 'Abel'. It sounds indescribably cute, an intimacy overdone, when they call him that, when they use that name, especially when it's uttered in the sweet little voice of five-year-old Eleonore, who looks exactly like Mrs Cornelius in photos of her as a child and whom the professor loves above all else.

'Little old chap,' says Ingrid kindly as she places her large but beautiful hand on the hand of her father, who presides not unnaturally over the family table in accordance with middle-class tradition. She has her place to his left, opposite her mother—'Good ancestor of mine, do please be reminded, because you've surely pushed it to the back of your mind. We're going to have a little bit of fun this afternoon, with goose-hopping[1] and herring salad—so what that means for your esteemed self is to keep calm and not despair, it will all be over by nine o'clock.'

'Is that so?' says Cornelius, making a longer face—'Good, good,' he says and shakes his head to show himself in harmony with what must be. 'I just thought—is it already Thursday? How time flies. So when are they coming?'

At half past four, answers Ingrid, whose brother usually leaves her to deal with their father: that's when our guests are due to arrive. If he stays upstairs he should hardly hear a thing, and from seven to eight is when he goes for a walk. If he wanted to, he could even escape across the terrace.

'Oh—' Cornelius says it in a way that means, 'You're exaggerating.' But then Bert steps in: 'It's the only evening of the week when Vanya isn't on stage. Every other evening he'd have to go at half past six. That really would be a blow to everyone in the party.'

'Vanya' is Ivan Herzl, the youthful, much-celebrated darling of the municipal theatre, a close friend of Bert and Ingrid, who often pops in for a cup of tea and visits him in his dressing room. He's an artist who, so it appears to the professor, stands on the stage in extremely mannered and unnatural balletic poses and shouts in agony. It's impossible for a professor of history to like that kind of thing, but Bert has given himself over powerfully to Herzl's influence, has taken to lining the lower edge of his eyelids with kohl, leading to a difficult but futile scene with his father, and, with a young person's insensitivity to the kind of feelings that hurt the scions of an older generation, has declared his intention not only to take Herzl as his model if he decides to become a dancer, but has in mind to adopt the same style should he become a waiter at The Cairo.

Cornelius, with his eyebrows slightly raised, wanting to show the understated loyalty and self-control that matter to his generation, bows lightly in the direction of his son. So far as anyone can see, the pantomime is free of irony and generally well meant. Bert might well see it as much in relation to himself as to his artist friend's powers of expression.

So who else is coming, the head of the household inquires. Various names come his way, some he knows better than others, people from the newly built villas, people from within the town, the names of Ingrid's fellow pupils from the top class of the girls' Gymnasium... There are a few people on his list they haven't contacted yet. Max, for example, is someone they still need to telephone, Max Hergesell, student of engineering, as Ingrid at once pronounces his name in the drawn-out, nasal fashion that she claims is the way all the Hergesells speak in private, and continues to imitate in so grippingly funny and lifelike a way that her parents are in danger of choking on their ghastly pudding because they are laughing so much. For even in times such as these people have to laugh when they find something amusing.

Every now and again the telephone rings in their father's study and the grown-up children run to answer it, because they know it's for them. Prices have been going up so much that a lot of people have had to give up the telephone, but the Corneliuses have just been able to hang on to theirs, just as they've so far hung on to their villa, built before the war, thanks to, though it's a sum barely adequate to the times, those millions that the professor receives as a lecturer in history. Their suburban house is elegant and comfortable, if rather neglected, because the shortage of materials makes repairs impossible; and also somewhat disfigured by the long pipes of the iron stoves. It is in the old upper-middle-class standard of living that they persist, but that's no longer appropriate, and, in a word, their lives are impoverished and difficult, and they wear worn-out clothes mended to make do. The children have never known anything else, this is the norm for them, the order of their lives; they are born proletarians living in a villa. The business of clothes bothers them hardly at all. They've invented a way of dressing that is appropriate to the times, the product of poverty and a taste for the Boy Scouts, something that in summer consists of barely more than a belted linen tunic and sandals. Scions of the old bourgeoisie find it harder.

The Grown-Ups chat next door with their friends while their napkins dangle from the arms of their chairs. It's people they've invited who are telephoning. They want to accept or decline or discuss something, and the Grown-Ups conduct the discussion in the slang they use in their circle, a mishmash of unusual coinages and high spirits, of which the Old Folk rarely understand a word. Meanwhile, the latter do have a view on what hospitality the guests will be offered. The professor exudes bourgeois pride. For supper, after an Italian salad[2] and open sandwiches on black bread, he wants there to be a rich layer cake, or something of the sort; but Frau Cornelius says that would be going too far—the young people don't expect it at all, is her view, and the children agree with her as they enjoy second helpings of the pudding.

The lady of the house, whom Ingrid takes after physically, though she's grown taller, has been left stressed and dispirited by the crazy difficulties besetting the household budget. She needs to get hold of a bath, but with the floor shifting under their feet, and everything all over the place, that's not doable for the time being. She thinks of the eggs that absolutely must be bought today and mentions it: the six-thousand-mark eggs, only available on this particular day of the week at a particular shop, a quarter of an hour away, and only being sold in limited quantities, which the children must set off to fetch immediately after the meal before all else. Danny, the neighbour's son, will come and pick them up and Xaver, in civvies, will also go along. For the shop will only give five eggs a week to a single household, and so the young people will enter the shop individually, go in one by one and use various assumed names, in order to secure a total of twenty eggs for the Villa Cornelius: a matter of huge fun every week for all concerned, not excluding the *muzhik* Kleinsgütl, but also expressly for Ingrid and Bert, who are so extraordinarily inclined to mystify their fellow human beings and lead them astray, and who do things like this at every turn purely for the sake of it, even when it's not a matter of eggs. In the tram they like to present themselves as quite different young people from those they actually are, so they speak to each other in a rural dialect they don't even know, they enjoy long, fake conversations in public, the kind of down-to-earth conversations ordinary people engage in: straightforward everyday stuff about politics and the price of food, and about non-existent people, so that the whole tramcar listens in on their exceedingly conventional chinwagging, feeling at once sympathetic and suspecting darkly that something isn't right. They then become ever more impudent and start to tell the most appalling stories about those non-existent people. Ingrid is quite capable of putting on a high, uneven, chirruping voice that sounds common and of passing herself off as a shop girl who has an illegitimate child, a son with a sadistic temperament who recently so indescribably mutilated a cow that a Christian could hardly bear to look at it. The way she chirrups the word 'mutilated' brings Bert close to exploding, but he manages to present a face of horrified sympathy to the world, and enters into a long conversation with the unfortunate shop girl that is at once gruesome, off-colour and stupid, talking about the nature of pathological cruelty, until finally an old man, sitting diagonally opposite them, carrying his ticket folded between his index finger and his signet ring, has had enough of it and complains publicly that people of such a tender age should not broach in such detail these *themata* (he uses the Greek plural for 'themes'). Whereupon Ingrid makes as if she's about to dissolve in tears, and Bert gives the impression he's only just managing to keep control of himself and suppress, with the greatest effort, using a power of will that might not hold him back for much longer, the deadly rage he feels towards the old man: he sits there with his fists clenched, grinding his teeth and trembling in his whole body, so that the old man, who had meant nothing but good, hastily leaves the carriage at the next stop.

This is the way the Grown-Ups amuse themselves. The telephone plays a prominent role in their doings: they ring up just about anyone, opera singers, civil servants and ministers of the Church, speaking as a shop girl or as the Count and Countess CornyHorny, and find it difficult to accept that they have the wrong number. Once they opened their parents' box of visiting cards and posted them here and there, but not so randomly that they didn't make a confusing half-sense, through the letter boxes of the neighbourhood, which gave rise to a great deal of consternation, since God knows who seemed suddenly to have announced they were visiting God knows whom.

Xaver, now without his white serving gloves, the yellow chain ring on his left hand visible, enters, flicking his hair back, to clear the table, and as the professor drinks up his eight-thousand-mark glass of low-alcohol lager and lights a cigarette, the Little Ones can be heard playing in the hall and on the stairs. As usual they come after the meal to greet their parents, storm into the dining room, battling with the door, both of them hanging on to the handle with their little hands, and tramping and tripping across the carpet on their hasty, uncertain legs, in red felt slippers with their socks hanging down in folds over them, calling out, chattering and giving some account or other, as each makes for their customary goal: Beißer towards his mother, climbing knees-first into her lap, to tell her how much he has eaten, and showing her his swollen tummy as proof, and Lorchen to her Abel—he so much her own because she is so much his own, because she feels the overwhelming tenderness in which he envelops her essence of being a little girl, feels that, like all deep sympathy, it is somewhat melancholy. Smiling, she relishes his love, in the way he gazes at her and kisses her finely formed little hand or her temples, with their tiny blueish veins showing through so delicately. They touch his heart. He dotes on her.

The children exude a distinct similarity to each other, yet one that is hard to pin down. Their clothes are roughly the same and their haircuts are similar, such that they really look like brother and sister. But they also differ radically from each other in the sense of being masculine and feminine. To speak plainly, this is a little Adam and this is a little Eve, something that for Beißer's part he seems to be conscious of and which contributes to his self-awareness; in his build alone he is stockier, sturdier, stronger, and what also underlines his four-year-old identity as a man is his manner, his face and his tone of voice, the way that he lets his little arms hang down athletically from slightly raised shoulders like a young American, and how, when he speaks, he draws his mouth down in an effort to achieve a deep and respectable timbre. Note in passing that all this dignified masculinity is more something he seeks than definitively finds in his nature; for, cherished and born in a time of devastating destruction, he's acquired an irritable nervous system than makes him distinctly edgy, he suffers terribly whenever he gets a glimpse of life's dark places, is inclined to wild rages and surges of fury and to desperate and bitter outbursts of tears over trivial things, and for that reason is already rather cosseted by his mother. He has round, chestnut-brown eyes that have a slight astigmatism—he'll probably soon need to wear prescription glasses—and a tiny long nose and a small mouth. They are the nose and the mouth of his father, which has become all the more obvious now that the professor has got rid of his beard and goes about clean-shaven. (He really couldn't keep the goatee any longer; even an historical person must in the end agree to accept the conventions of the present day.) But Cornelius has his little daughter on his knee, his baby Eleonore, his little Eve—so much more graceful than the boy and sweeter in her manner of speaking—and, holding his cigarette far away from her, he lets her finger his glasses with her fine little hands, glasses divided into lenses for reading and lenses for distance and which every day excite her curiosity anew.

Fundamentally he feels that his wife's preference rests on a nobler feeling than his own and that Beißer's troubled masculinity is more demanding than his more easy-going little one's loving charm. Yet you can't dictate to the heart what it should feel, he tells himself, and his heart has belonged to his little girl ever since she existed, since the first time he saw her. He remembers that first occasion almost whenever he holds her in his arms; it was in a bright room in the maternity clinic where Lorchen came into the world, at a twelve-year gap from her older siblings. He walked in and the mother smiled almost in that same moment when he gingerly pulled back the curtain from the heavenly little doll's bed which stood beside the big one and caught sight of the little miracle that lay there in the pillows, so beautifully formed and so sweetly proportioned that a kind of clarity emanated from her, with tiny hands which, as a minute version of what they would become, were already as beautiful now; he noticed how with her wide-open sky-blue eyes, as they were then, she reflected back the brightness of the day—and almost from the first moment he felt himself caught and bound fast; it was love at first sight and forever, a feeling that was unknown, unexpected and unhoped for—did consciousness of it even come into question—a feeling that, when it took possession of him, with surprise and joy he immediately recognized as what Life was about; what mattered.

Note in passing that Doctor Cornelius, when he thinks about it carefully, knows there's something not quite right about that feeling being entirely unanticipated and never even hoped for; not quite right to say it's an involuntary feeling over which the human mind has no power. Fundamentally he understands that it didn't just overwhelm him from nowhere and put him in touch with his vital core; rather that unconsciously he was prepared or, more correctly, that something had prepared him; something in him was ready to discover that feeling at the given moment, and his capacity as a professor of history was exactly that something, so very strange as it might seem to say. Not that Doctor Cornelius does say it, but, secretly smiling, he knows it from time to time. He knows that professors of history don't love history insofar as it happens, but because it has happened; that they hate the present chaos because they experience it as disconnected, anarchic and an assault on their discipline, 'unhistorical' in a word, and that their heart belongs to the coherent and historical past they can revere. For, as this university man tells himself on his walk beside the river before dinner, an atmosphere of timelessness and eternity surrounds the past, and this is the atmosphere an agitated university professor finds much more congenial than the irreverent outbursts of the present day. The past is eternalized, which means it is dead, and death is the source of everything we revere and can make sense of. The Herr Doktor has this private insight as he walks in the dark. It was his sense of continuity, his instinct for 'the eternal', that sought relief from the shamelessness of the times in his love for his little daughter. For a father's love and a child at its mother's breast, those things are timeless and eternal and therefore most sacred and beautiful. And yet in the dark Cornelius understands that there is something not quite right and good about this love of his—he admits it to himself theoretically, for the sake of science. In its origins this love has something skewed about it, an enmity at its heart. That love does not side with the present moment in which Life happens; it sides with what is already over, namely death. Yes, strange as it seems, that's true, up to a point. His passion for this sweet little bundle of life propagated from himself has something to do with death, it clings to him, against Life, and in a certain sense that's not at all fine and good—although it would be a demented act of asceticism to tear this most beautiful and pure feeling from his heart because of a scientific insight he happened to stumble across.

He's holding his little daughter on his lap, she with her little pink legs dangling down over his knees, and he's talking to her, his eyebrows raised, his tone one of tender and reverent homage, though he's jesting, of course, and then he's listening in return to the sweet, high little voice in which she answers him and calls him Abel. All the while he's exchanging questioning looks with the children's mother, who is soothing Beißer and, by way of a gentle reproach, trying to get him to pull himself together and see reason, because today life has so riled him that he has succumbed once again to a bout of rage and has behaved like a howling dervish. Now and again Cornelius also looks somewhat suspiciously across at the Grown-Ups, for he finds it perfectly possible that the particular scientific insights he enjoys on his evening walks are not entirely alien to them either. Although if that is the case they don't show it. Standing behind their chairs, their hands resting on the arms, they survey the scene of parental happiness indulgently, but also with a touch of irony.

The children wear thick, brick-red little artists' smocks, embroidered in a modern fashion, which belonged to Bert and Ingrid in their time and which are exactly the same, the sole difference being that with Beißer tiny short trousers show beneath the tunic. They have the same haircut too, a pageboy style. Beißer's hair is blond but unevenly so, beset with patches that are slowly growing darker, and it's untidily overgrown all over, unkempt and looks like a funny little wig that doesn't fit. By contrast Lorchen's hair is chestnut-brown, as fine as silk, shiny and as delightful as her whole little person. It covers her ears, which as everyone knows are not the same size: one is perfectly proportioned, the other a bit distorted, quite clearly too big. Her father sometimes pulls the ears forwards, marvelling over them in the strongest terms, as if he had never noticed this tiny failing before, which both amuses Lorchen and embarrasses her. Her wide-set eyes are golden-brown and have a sweet shimmer, a look of great clarity and love. The brows above them are blonde. Her nose is still quite formless, with rather thick nostrils, so that the holes are almost round like circles, and her mouth is large and expressive, with a beautifully curved and supple upper lip. When she laughs and shows her pearly-white teeth with a gap in between (she's only lost one; wiggling it in all directions she got her father

98

to give it a final twist, whereupon she grew very pale and shaky), she gets little dimples in her cheeks that owe their characteristic, somewhat concave shape, despite their childlike softness, to the fact that the lower half of her face is just a tiny bit prominent. On one cheek, close to the hairline, she has a fluffy mole.

Overall she herself doesn't much like her appearance—a sign that she bothers about it. Her verdict is that her little face is, alas, definitely quite ugly, while her little 'figure' is really nice. She likes carefully chosen, educated snippets of speech and uses them all one after another, like 'perhaps, that may very well be, in the end'. Beißer's self-critical worries are more concerned with moral issues. He's inclined to contrition, considers himself a great sinner because of his rages, and is convinced he won't go to Heaven but will end up in 'hell'. When people respond by saying that God possesses a great deal of insight and knows what it is to be five years old, in deep depression he only shakes his head with its mop of hair like an ill-fitting wig and declares that it's impossible for him ever to be saved. If he gets a cold, rheum seems to engulf him entirely; he's rasping and croaking from head to foot, if he has even a hint of it, and immediately gets a high temperature that leaves him sniffing and snorting. Nannie-Annie turns straight away to the dark arts to explain his constitution, and is of the opinion that a boy with such 'unusually thick blood' could have a stroke at any time.

Once she thought this terrible moment had already come: when, to atone for having gone berserk, Beißer had been made to stand in the corner with his face to the wall, and then when someone checked on him they found that his face had gone completely blue, far bluer than Nannie-Annie's own. She caused turmoil in the house when she announced that the boy's excessively thick blood had just brought about his very last hour, and to his own justified surprise naughty Beißer found himself suddenly enveloped in

99

anxiety and tenderness, until it was found that the blue on his skin was not the result of a blocked artery but the paint on the wall of the nursery, its indigo having rubbed off on his tear-stained face.

She too came into the nursery and stood in the doorway with her hands together in a white apron, with greasy hair, hooded eyes and the look of one whose dignified self-regard revealed her limitations. 'It's marvellous,' she said, proud of her care and instruction, 'how children sort themselves out.' She'd recently had seventeen rotten teeth removed and had false teeth made of the same yellow, with red rubber gums, and these now embellished her peasant face.

Somehow the peculiar idea got into her mind that her teeth were the subject of widespread discussion, as if sparrows were chirping it from the rooftops. 'There's been a lot of pointless talk on the occasion of my getting myself, as everyone knows, fitted with false teeth,' she averred with a kind of mystical severity. Generally she tends to an obscure, unclear manner of speaking that others find hard to understand, for example speaking of a Doctor Bleifuß; every child knows who that is, she says, and 'There are others living in this house,' she says, 'who pretend to be him.' It's the sort of utterance one can only greet with a nod of the head and then go on one's way. She teaches the children lovely poems, for example:

> Choo-choo train, choo-choo, choo choo,
> Engine-driver's mate, choo choo.
> Sounds his whistle, parp'dy parp,
> Now we're timely, sharp as sharp.

Or one of those week-in-the-kitchen rhymes, this one full of things there won't be left tomorrow, appropriately enough for the present day, but also full of fun:

> Monday's when the week begins
> Tuesday's getting short of things
> Wednesday's child is full of woe
> Thursday, I'd say, just so-so.
> Friday now it's fish for lunch.
> Saturday we're quite a bunch.
> Sunday's pork 'n' taters roast
> That's the food we love the most.

Or a peculiar, indescribably romantic quatrain full of unsolved mystery:

> Open the gate, open the gate,
> Make way for a lovely coach.
> Who sits in the lovely coach?
> A Lord with a golden brooch.

Or, finally, the ballads of little Maria, with their terrible rhymes, Maria who sat on a rock, on a rock, on a rock and combed her equally golden hair, her golden hair, her golden hair. And of Rudolf who drew a knife, drew a knife, drew out a knife, and the little girl came to a terrible end.

Lorchen recites and sings all this most charmingly, with her quick-fire little mouth and her sweet voice—much better than Beißer. She does everything better than he does and he truly admires her, sees himself as second-best in everything, despite his attacks of revulsion and noisy bursts of anger. She often helps him acquire knowledge, she takes him through the birds in the picture book and gives them names: the cloud-eater, the hail-eater, the raven-eater. He has to say the names after her. She teaches him medicine too, instructs him in the names of illnesses such as chest inflammation, blood inflammation and breathing inflammation. Whenever he doesn't pay attention and can't say it after her she puts him in the corner. Once she even slapped him, but then she felt so ashamed that she put herself in the corner for a good few hours.

Yes indeed, they get on well, bound to each other heart and soul. They go through everything together, every adventure. They get home and, both talking at once, and now as then still terribly excited, they tell the story of how they have seen 'two moo-cows and a veal' on the high road. With the servants downstairs—with Xaver and the Hinterhöfer ladies, two ladies who once were middle-class now work on an au pair basis, as people say, that is they perform the functions of cook and chambermaid in exchange for board and lodging—they get on like a house on fire, and detect from time to time an affinity between the relationship of these lower-ranked people to their parents and their own. If they get told off, they head for the kitchen and say: 'Our olders and betters are in a foul mood!' Still it's more fun to play with the people upstairs and particularly with Abel when he doesn't have to do his reading and writing. More strange and fantastic ideas occur to him than they do to Xaver and the ladies. The two children have a game they play which means going for a walk as 'four men'. Abel bends his knees so deeply that he makes himself as small as they are, and joins them on their walk, holding their hands, and they never want the game to end. As five men altogether, including Abel who has made himself so tiny, they could go round and round the dining room all day.

Then there's the hugely thrilling cushion game, whereby one of the children, usually Lorchen, goes and sits on his chair at the dining table and, as if Abel hasn't noticed, waits as still as a mouse for him to come. He approaches slowly, looking up at the ceiling and talking to himself in such a way as to suggest he's really looking forward to sitting in his comfy chair, and then he sits on Lorchen. 'Heh!' he says. 'What's this?' And he shuffles himself this way and that, without hearing the suppressed giggling that's going on behind him. 'Someone's put a cushion on my chair! Why's it so hard and uneven and lumpy? Just my luck to have to sit on something so uncomfortable!' With that he moves about more and more frantically on the unfamiliar cushion, and feels his way into the enchanted giggling and squeaking going on behind him, until he finally turns round and the drama ends with a great scene of discovery and reconciliation. They can repeat this game too a hundred times and it loses none of its excitement and charm.

There's no time for fun like this today. The Grown-Ups' forthcoming party, a nuisance, dominates the atmosphere, and before it starts there is who gets what shopping to settle: Lorchen has newly recited 'Choo-choo train, choo-choo train' and Doctor Cornelius has just discovered, to her great shame, that one ear is quite markedly bigger than the other, when Danny, the neighbour's son, arrives to pick up Bert and Ingrid; meanwhile Xaver has changed out of his striped uniform into an ordinary suit, which though he's rather squeezed into it immediately gives him an attractive, even racy look. So then the Little Ones repair to their realm upstairs with Nannie-Annie, while the professor withdraws to his study to read, as is his habit after meals, and his wife turns her active attention to the little anchovy rolls and the Italian salad which are to be prepared for the dancing party. Before the young people arrive she has to cycle into town with her shopping bag to exchange for groceries the sum of money she has in her hand, and which she needs to spend before it loses its value.[3]

Cornelius is sitting back in his chair and reading. With his cigar between his index finger and his middle finger, he's reading something in Macaulay about the debts the English state ran up towards the end of the seventeenth century, and then in a book by some French writer about Spain's increasing debt towards the end of the sixteenth—both things for his lecture tomorrow morning. He wants to compare England's extraordinary economic prosperity in those times with the disastrous effects which state debt set in motion in Spain a hundred years earlier, and analyse the ethical and psychological causes of this difference. That will give him an opportunity to move from the England of William III, which is the time in question, to the age of Philip II and the Counter-Reformation, which is his personal hobby horse and on which he has written an admirable book—a work much cited, and to which he owes his teaching position. As his cigar burns down and weighs rather heavily in his fingers, he comes up with a couple of sentences tinged with melancholy that he will run past his students tomorrow, on the tardy Philip's fundamentally hopeless struggle with the new, on, throughout the course of history, those forces of the individual and the Germanic way with freedom that undo empires, and on the struggle that Life has rejected and therefore God too has condemned—of a traditional nobility against the powers of progress and transformation. He finds the sentences good and can't resist polishing them as he puts the books he has used back on the shelves, then he goes up to his bedroom to give his day its usual caesura. He needs to spend an hour with his eyes closed and shutters drawn. It's a standard requirement of his after excursions into learned matters. But it will be interpreted today as a sign of the interrupted domestic arrangements. His heart beats a touch faster when he suddenly remembers the party to come, and that makes him smile; in his head the sentences he has in mind for the morrow merge with Philip dressed in black silk and the ball the children have arranged at home, and like this he falls asleep for five minutes.

As he lies there and rests he repeatedly hears the doorbell ring and the garden gate close, and each time he experiences a little tremor of excitement, expectation and anxiety at the thought that the young people have started arriving and are crowding into the hall they will use as a dance floor. Each time over again he smiles at that tremor, but then his smile is also a sign of nervous excitement, which of course also contains an element of pleasure; for who doesn't look forward to a party. He gets up at half past four (it is already evening) and freshens up at the washstand. The basin has been broken for a year now. It is a bowl made to tilt, but the fixture has broken away on one side and it can't be repaired because no one will come to do the job, and it can't be replaced because no manufacturer is in a position to supply a new one.[4] To make do it's been hung on the edges of the marble tabletop over its waste pipe and you can only empty it by lifting it up with two hands and pouring the water out. As he does several times every day, Cornelius shakes his head over the basin, but then takes particular care finishing his preparations; beneath the ceiling light he polishes his glasses until they are perfectly shiny and transparent—and then he goes along the corridor and down to the dining room.

On the way he hears the voices intermingling and the gramophone, which is already playing, and his face composes itself into a suitably sociable attitude. 'Please don't mind me!' he determines he will say while heading straight towards tea in the dining room. The sentence strikes him as the right one for the moment: outwardly cheerily considerate, as indeed it is, while for himself suitable armour in his defence.

The hall is brightly lit: every electric bulb in the candelabra is blazing, apart from one that has gone. Cornelius stops and stands on one of the lower steps of the stairs and surveys the hall. It's a pretty room in this light, with the Marées[5] copy over the brick fireplace, the panelling, which is incidentally softwood, and the red carpet, on which the guests are standing about chatting, holding cups of tea and half-slices of bread spread with anchovy paste. A party atmosphere, a faint perfume of clothes, hair and breath wafts through the hall, characteristic and memorable. The door to the cloakroom is open, for more guests are still to come.

Social gatherings are dazzling in the first moment; the professor can only see the general picture. He hasn't noticed that Ingrid, in a dark silk dress with a pleated white bolero and bare arms, is standing close to him with friends at the foot of the stairs. She nods and smiles up at him with her fine teeth.

'Had a good rest?' she asks quietly, between themselves, and as he recognizes her with a kind of surprise and what he feels he can't reconcile with being her father, she introduces him to her friends.

'May I introduce Herr Zuber?' she says. 'This is Fräulein Plaichinger.'

Herr Zuber strikes him as skinny, but the Plaichinger girl by contrast is a real Germanic type, blonde, voluptuous and loosely dressed, with a snub nose and the high voice of a heavily built woman, as becomes apparent when she answers the professor's studiedly polite greeting.

'Oh, welcome, welcome,' he says. 'Lovely that you should honour us so. I suppose you're a fellow classmate?'

Herr Zuber is a member of Ingrid's golf club. He's in business, works as something in his uncle's brewery, and the professor exchanges a joke with him about the quality of low-alcohol beer, making it seem as if in that moment he's vastly exaggerating the influence of young Zuber on the quality of the beer. 'But please don't let me interrupt,' he says then and makes his way towards the dining room.

'Ah there's Max,' said Ingrid. 'Heh, Max, you slowcoach, where have you been? The party's in full swing and you're only just arriving.'

The young people all call each other '*du*'[6] and engage in an easy manner that is quite alien to the older generation; there's hardly a trace of gallantry and restraint, nor formal etiquette.

A young man with a white shirt front and a narrow evening bow tie comes over from the cloakroom to the staircase and offers his greetings—dark-haired but pink-cheeked, shaven, of course, but with a bit of beard growth beside his ears, a young man as pretty as a picture, not as absurdly and brazenly beautiful as a gypsy fiddler, but pretty in a very pleasant, civilized and winning fashion, with dark, friendly eyes and a dinner jacket that doesn't quite fit him.

'Now, now, Cornelia, my dear friend of the house of Cornelius, don't get cross with me. The idiotic institute,' he says; and Ingrid introduces him to her father as Herr Hergesell.

So that's Herr Hergesell then. As a well-brought-up young man he thanks the head of the household, who is shaking his hand, for the kind invitation. 'I've had to get my skates on,' he says and makes a little linguistic joke. 'It's quite bananas that today of all days I should have classes until four, and then I had to get home to change.' This brings him to speak of his dancing pumps, with which he's just had, as he tells it, quite an issue in the cloakroom.

'I brought them with me in a bag,' he recounts. 'It's just not right that we should trample your carpet in our outdoor shoes. But then, out of what confusion I don't know, I forgot to put in a shoehorn and God knows I just couldn't get into them, ha, ha, I mean, just imagine, what an unbelievable bind! I've not had such a narrow pair of pumps my whole life long. The sizes turn out different each time, you can't rely on them, and then these days the material is hard—look, you see, it's not leather, it's moulded iron. I got my whole index finger stuck in there.' And in rather too casual a fashion he holds up his red index finger for everyone to see, at the same time as he once more calls the whole thing 'a bind'; a ridiculous business, that's what it is. He really speaks the way Ingrid does when she imitates him, in a nasal voice with particular emphases, but apparently not with any affectation: that's just the way the Hergesells happen to speak.

Doctor Cornelius regrets that there isn't a shoehorn in the cloakroom, and carefully attends to the index finger. 'Now please don't let me spoil your party,' he says. 'Forgive me!' And he walks across the hall into the dining room.

There are guests in there too; the family dinner table has been extended, and people are drinking tea at it. But the professor goes straight to the corner with the nice little round table where he normally likes to drink his tea. It's covered with an embroidered cloth which gives it a special appeal. There he finds his wife talking to Bert and two other young men. One of them is Herzl; Cornelius knows him and greets him. The name of the other is Möller—a *Wandervogel* type who's taken up the fashion for the outdoors and who apparently doesn't have any clothes to suit the middle-class social calendar, and doesn't want to either (essentially that calendar doesn't exist any more). He's a young man who's not going to dress as one of the ruling class (that doesn't exist any more either) and is wearing a shirt with a belt and short trousers. He has a quiff, a long neck and horn-rimmed spectacles and the professor learns that he works for a bank, but that he also has an artistic interest in folklore, as a collector and singer of folk songs from every part of the world and in every tongue. Today he has his guitar with him too because someone asked him to bring it along. It's hanging in the cloakroom in a carrier made of waxed cloth.

Herzl the actor is small and slim, but with vigorous black whiskers, a sign of which is the amount of powder he's used in shaving. His eyes are exceedingly large, moist and deeply melancholy; at the same time, besides the excess of shaving powder he's also applied something red—the matt carmine on his cheekbones is evidently of cosmetic origin. That's peculiar, thinks the professor. You would think, wouldn't you, either melancholy or make-up. Together they form a psychological contradiction, surely. What make-up would a melancholic wear? But then we have the special, psychologically strange type of the artist and his soul, which makes this contradiction possible, maybe consists in being just that. That's interesting and there's no reason why it shouldn't occur. It's a legitimate type, an Ur-type... 'Help yourself to lemon, my dear man of the theatre, servant of the imperial court!'

There aren't any actors in the service of the imperial court any longer, but Herzl doesn't at all mind being called that, even though he's a revolutionary artist. That's another contradiction that lies deep in his soul and belongs to his psychological type. Quite rightly, the professor makes a lot of his presence and flatters him, somewhat to atone for the secret offence he took when he saw the light smudge of rouge on Herzl's cheeks.

'I am most deeply obliged to you, my esteemed Herr Professor!' says Herzl, so overcome that only his excellent diction can prevent him saying the wrong thing.[7] His behaviour in general to his young lady host and especially to the family of this house is so excessively respectful that it seems born of a quite exaggerated and self-deprecating politeness. It's as if he has a bad conscience because of the rouge which he was inwardly compelled to wear, but which he himself disapproves of, as if from within the heart of the professor himself, and with whom he longs to reconcile himself through his very great deference towards a world that does not wear cosmetics.

Over their cups of tea people are chatting about Möller's folk songs, about Spanish and Basque folk songs, and that brings them to new insights into Schiller's play *Don Carlos*, on at the municipal theatre and in which Herzl is playing the title role. He's talking about his Carlos. 'I do hope', he says, 'that my Carlos is something more than cobbled together.' There's a lot of criticism of everything else that's involved, of the production values, the venue, and all too soon the professor finds himself caught up in the wake, reminded of Spain's fate in the Counter-Reformation, and that seems to him almost embarrassing. He's totally innocent, he's done nothing to steer the conversation in this direction. He's afraid it might seem that he's taken the opportunity to give a lecture, it bothers him and he falls silent. He's glad when the Little Ones, Lorchen and Beißer, come to the table. They're in miniature outfits of blue velvet, their Sunday best, and want in their own way to be part of the gathering until bedtime. With great big eyes they shyly say 'Good Afternoon' to strangers and have to give their name and their age. Herr Möller looks upon them seriously, no more, but Herzl the actor puts on a show of being enthralled, enchanted and enraptured by them. He goes so far as to bless them, lifts his eyes to the ceiling and claps his hands together in front of his face. He surely means it sincerely, but his habit of producing what is needed for an effective performance on the stage makes his words and deeds appear frightfully false, and on top of that it seems as if his devotion to the children is another way of atoning for the rouge on his cheekbones.

There are no guests left at the tea table any more, and now that people are dancing in the hall the children run over there and the professor retreats. 'Have fun!' he says, shaking the hands of Herr Möller and Herzl as they pass by. 'Really, I mean it, have fun!' And he goes across into his study, the peaceful refuge he has created, lowers the blinds, switches on the desk lamp and sets himself to work.

It's the kind of work that, if there's a lot of disturbance, he can still do: a couple of letters, a couple of passages from his reading to take note of. Of course Cornelius is distracted. Little details stay in his mind, Herr Hergesell's stiff evening shoes, the high voice emanating from the Plaichinger girl's fat body. While he's writing or sitting back in his chair staring into space his thoughts return to Möller's collection of Basque folk songs, to Herzl's self-effacement and exaggeration, 'his' Carlos and the court of Philip II. He finds that conversation is a mysterious thing. It's susceptible, it can of itself easily take a turn in the direction of a preoccupation of which one is unaware. He's surely observed that many times, he thinks. Now and again he listens to the noise coming from the dance party beyond. It's hardly loud. All he can hear is people talking. There's no sound of feet gliding across the floor.

For that's just it: they don't circle and glide, they have a strange way of moving about the carpet which doesn't bother them, in quite a different state of mind from how it was in his day, moving to the sounds of the gramophone, sounds he finds hard to keep up with, these strange orphans of the new world, the instrumentation jazzed up, with every kind of percussion, which the machine enhances as it reproduces it, and the sharp clicking of castanets, but which function as jazz instruments here and don't seem at all Spanish. No, not Spanish at all. And that brings him back to his professional train of thought.

After half an hour he gets the idea that it would be no more than friendly of him to contribute to the pleasures of the party with a box of cigarettes. It's not right, he finds, for the young people to have to smoke their own cigarettes—although they themselves would hardly give it a second thought. And he goes into the empty dining room and takes from a cupboard on the wall containing his store a box, not exactly of the best, or, rather, not those he himself prefers to smoke, a variety rather too long and thin, which he doesn't mind using this opportunity to get rid of, for they're only young people, after all. He carries the box with him into the hall, raises it up with a smile and then leaves it open on the mantelpiece, only then to slip straight back into his room with hardly a glance around him.

Just now there's a break in the dancing and the music machine is quiet. People are sitting and standing around at the edges of the hall, chatting, at the map table in front of the windows, on the chairs in front of the fireplace. Youngsters are also sitting on the carpeted stairs, on a thick-pile runner which has worn menacingly thin, and the effect is of an amphitheatre: Max Hergesell, for instance, is sitting there with the ample Plaichinger girl with her high-pitched voice; she's staring into his face while he's talking to her almost lying down, with one elbow behind him resting on the step above and the other hand gesticulating as he speaks. The centre of the room is empty except for, right in the middle, the two Little Ones in their blue costumes, clumsily intertwined, quietly, slowly and carefully taking a turn. Cornelius bends down to them as he passes and strokes their hair, saying something nice, without interrupting their solemn little enterprise. But reaching his door he sees Hergesell, the engineering student, probably because he has noticed the professor, push himself up from the step with his elbow, come down and take Lorchen out of her brother's arms in order to dance with her himself in droll fashion, without music. He looks just like Cornelius when the aforementioned does his four-men walk. His knees deeply bent at the same time as trying to hold her like a grown woman, he takes a few shimmy steps with an embarrassed Lorchen. It's very amusing for anyone who notices it. It's a sign to switch the gramophone back on and for all the dancing to begin again. With his hand on the doorknob the professor looks on for a moment, nodding, his shoulders twitch with laughter, and then he goes into his room. For several minutes his face mechanically retains the smile he wore outside.

Again he searches among his papers beside the desk lamp. He writes something, deals with a few simple tasks. After a while he notices that the company has moved from the hall to his wife's sitting room, which is connected both to the hall and his own room. Now there's talking in there and the sounds of a guitar mixed up with it, as if trying to catch people's attention. Herr Möller intends to sing, it turns out, and he has a good voice. The young civil servant strums resonantly on the guitar and sings in his powerful bass voice a song in a foreign language—it may be that it's Swedish; by the end, an end which is received with great applause, the professor still can't recognize it for certain. There's a heavy curtain behind the door to the sitting room that dampens the sound. As a new song begins, Cornelius creeps out.

It's half-dark in the sitting room. The only light on is a standard lamp with a shade, and there nearby sits Möller cross-legged on the wooden pouffe, plucking the strings with his thumb. The audience isn't assembled in any particular way, it has the feel of having been carelessly improvised, since there aren't enough seats for so many people to sit on. Some are standing, but many, young women also among them, are simply sitting on the floor, with their arms around their knees or their legs stretched out in front of them. Hergesell, for example, even though he's in evening dress, sits on the floor like that, at the foot of the grand piano, with the Plaichinger girl next to him. The Little Ones are there too: Frau Cornelius, in an armchair opposite the singer, is holding them both on her lap, and the barbarian Beißer has begun talking loudly in the middle of the singing, so that he has to be stopped with hushing and finger-wagging. Lorchen would never get herself into trouble like that; she stays gentle and quiet on her mother's knee. The professor tries to catch her eye, so he can make a hidden sign to his little daughter; but she doesn't see him, although she doesn't appear to be looking at the singer either. Her eyes go deeper.

Möller is singing the 'Joli tambour':

Sire, mon roi, donnez-moi votre fille [8]

Everyone is enraptured. 'He is good!' people hear Hergesell say, in that nasal, as if aiming to be peculiarly fastidious, way common to all the Hergesells, then there's something German to follow, for which Herr Möller himself has composed the melody, and which is greeted with passionate applause on the part of the young people, a beggar's song:

> Beggar-lass will go to church,
> Yayyouchay!
> Beggar-man will tag along,
> Tiddletumteetay

After the jolly beggar's song a mood of nothing less than exulta-tion prevails. 'He's really exceptionally good!' says Hergesell again, in that way of his. There's something Hungarian next, another winning number, presented in the wildly alien original language, and Möller has enormous success. The professor too visibly joins in the applause. This intrusion into the jazz party of high culture and of someone practising an art form revived from yesterday lifts his heart. He goes up to Möller, congratulates him and chats with him about the stuff of his performance, his sources, a songbook with the music, which Möller promises to lend him for inspection. Cornelius is all the more affectionate towards him in the way that he, like all fathers, immediately compares the gifts and values of this young person, who is a stranger, with those of his own son, and he feels discontent, envy and shame as he does so. And to think that this Möller holds down a job in a bank! (He has no idea whether Möller is really so good at his job in the bank.) And to think that as well as his job he can boast this special talent, which has naturally required some energy and study to bring it to fruition. Contrast him with my poor Bert, who knows nothing and can do nothing, and only thinks of playing the fool, although he surely doesn't have a talent for that either! He wants to be fair, tries telling himself that Bert is still a fine lad, with more resources perhaps than the successful Möller, that perhaps there's a poet in him waiting to emerge, or something of that ilk, and that his plans to be the kind of waiter who is so nimble he could work as a dancer are just boyish fantasies, something to do with the distorted times. But his pessimism and envy as a father are stronger. As Möller starts singing again Doctor Cornelius goes back to his study.

It's just coming up to seven o'clock, and with his attention half elsewhere he sets to as before; and since he remembers a short business letter which he can very well write now, the hour moves on to half past seven—for writing is time-consuming. Half past eight is when they're serving the Italian salad, so the professor had better go out now, put his letter in the postbox and get his quota of fresh air and exercise in the winter dark. The dance in the hall resumed ages ago; he has to pass through to get to his coat and outdoor shoes, but that doesn't cause him anxiety any more: he's just one of the hosts who keeps cropping up in a room full of partying young people and he doesn't have to fear he'll be in the way. He steps out of his room, after he's put his papers away and picked up his letters, but then loses his urgency to leave the hall they're using as a ballroom when he find his wife sitting in an armchair close by the door of his study.

She's sitting there and watching, visited now and again by the Grown-Ups and other young people, and Cornelius comes and stands beside her and watches with a similar smile what's going on, as the lively event seems to be coming to a head. There are other spectators: Blue Anna, a buttoned-up, dowdy figure, is standing beside the stairs, because the Little Ones can't get enough of the festivities and because she must take care that Beißer doesn't leap about and make himself dizzy and stir his all-too-thick blood into a state of dangerous excitement. But then the people from below stairs too want a part in the dance that the Grown-Ups are enjoying: not only the Hinterhöfer ladies but also Xaver are standing at the door next to the kitchen annexe where the food was prepared and enjoying watching. Fräulein Walburga, the older of the two sisters fallen beneath their social class, is the one who does the cooking (not to call her straight out a cook, which she doesn't like to hear). She watches with her brown eyes through thick, round spectacles which have a tiny little piece of linen wrapped around the bridge so that it doesn't pinch. She's an agreeable type with a sense of humour. Meanwhile Fräulein Cecilia, the younger one, though not exactly young any more, has the look on her face, as usual, of being a woman of means. This look is a way of preserving her dignity as a former member of the third estate. Fräulein Cecilia suffers bitterly from having fallen from the sphere of the petty bourgeoisie down into the servant class. She refuses point-blank to wear a little cap or any other sign of the occupation of chambermaid, and her worst hour comes regularly every Wednesday evening when Xaver has time off and she has to wait at table. She does the job with her face averted and her nose in the air, a deposed queen; it's a torture and really quite oppressive to have to witness her humiliation, and when it once happened that the Little Ones came for the evening meal, they both simultaneously burst into tears at the sight of her.

The lad who goes by the name of Xaver is not suffering anything of this kind. He really likes serving at table, and does it with a certain aplomb which is both natural and because he has been trained, for he was once an apprentice waiter. Otherwise he's really a thoroughly useless layabout and a charlatan, with positive qualities which his modest employers are always ready to concede, but an impossible charlatan all the same. You have to take him as you find him, and not ask for figs from thorns.[9] He is the child and fruit of the loose times we live in, a perfect example of his generation, an amiable Bolshevik. The professor likes to call him 'the steward of the show', because he always stands his ground in unusual and amusing circumstances and presents himself as helpful and amenable. Yet, entirely unacquainted with the notion of duty as he is, it's no easier to get him to fulfil regular, boring, everyday requirements than it is to get some dogs to jump over a stick. Apparently it would be against his nature, against which it's difficult to have a case. If there were a particular, unusual and amusing reason to do so he would be ready to get out of bed at any hour of the night you chose. On a daily basis, however, he doesn't get up before eight o'clock—he won't do it, he won't jump over the stick; but all day long the signs of his relaxed existence, his playing his mouth organ, the sound of his rough singing voice, full of feeling, his merry whistling make their way from the kitchen below to the upper floors, the smoke from his cigarettes fills the room where the food is prepared. He stops and watches the loose women who have fallen beneath their original status. In the morning, while the professor is having breakfast, he tears the date off his desk calendar—otherwise he touches nothing in the room. He should leave the calendar alone, Doctor Cornelius has often instructed him, because he's inclined to tear off two leaves at once and so run the risk of getting into a complete mess. But young Xaver likes the task of tearing off the page of the calendar and won't let it be denied him for that reason.

It should also be noted that he's a lover of children, which is one of his winning traits. He gives his all to playing with the Little Ones in the garden, has a talent for cutting things out and sticking them together and even reads aloud to them, with his thick lips, from their books, which is pretty fantastic to hear. He's a passionate lover of the cinema and is often overcome with melancholy and dreaming, he talks to himself, after he's seen a film. Vague hopes of one day personally belonging to this world and finding his happiness there keep him going. His hopes show in the way he flicks his hair, in his bodily agility and his daring. He has a fondness for climbing the ash tree in the front garden, which is a tall tree that bends from side to side; he nips from branch to branch right up to the very top, and everyone watching gets worried and anxious. Up there he lights a cigarette and sways back and forth so that the tall mast trembles in its very roots, and keeps an eye out for a cinema director who might come along and hire him.

Were he to take off his striped jacket and put on ordinary clothes he could easily join in the dancing; he wouldn't stand out particularly. The people who are friends with the Grown-Ups are of varied appearance: the middle-class business suit turns up frequently among the young people, but it doesn't predominate; those of a similar type to Möller the song-man are well represented, as much on the female side as among the young men. Standing beside his wife's chair and watching the proceedings, the professor knows the social circumstances of the younger generation indirectly, through what he's heard. They are girls from the Gymnasium, women students and textile-workers; on the male side they are adventurous and sometimes completely invented existences, products of the times. A pale, lanky youth with pearls in his shirt, the son of a dentist, is none other than a speculator on the stock exchange and has ended up living, so the professor has heard, like Aladdin with his magic lamp. He owns a car, treats his friends to champagne suppers and likes whenever he can to buy them presents, choice little gifts of gold and mother-of-pearl. He's also brought presents for his young hosts today: a gold pencil for Bert and for Ingrid an enormous pair of earrings, rings of a really barbaric size but which thank God are meant not to be pulled through the earlobe but fastened over the top of it with a clip. The Grown-Ups laugh as they come over and show their presents to their parents, and the latter shake their heads, looking upon them with astonishment, while Aladdin takes repeated bows in the distance.

The young people put everything into their dancing, insofar as it can be called dancing; they happily abandon themselves to it. The way they hold each other and the position of their bodies is quite new, with the lower body pressed forwards, the shoulders lifted and the hips swaying, following a set of instructions that is difficult to discern, as they move slowly around on the carpet, not tiring, because it's impossible to get tired like this. There are no bosoms rising and falling, no burning cheeks to be seen. Here and there two young girls are dancing together, and even occasionally two young men; they don't mind one way or the other. They dance to the exotic sounds of the gramophone, which is furnished with a strong needle so that it plays loudly, and everyone can hear its shimmies, foxtrots and one-steps, the double foxy, the African shimmy, the Java dances and Creole polkas—wild, perfumed stuff, now languid, now intense, with a strange rhythm, a monotonous tone, Negro music whipped up into something new with fancy orchestration, drums, jingling and clicking.

'What's the name of the record?' Cornelius asks, as Ingrid sweeps by with the pale speculator. The tune he has in mind is strikingly languid and intense and affects him directly, puts him in exactly that mood, he notices.

'The Prince of Pappenheim, Rest Easy, My Lovely Child,' she says, and smiles fondly with her white teeth.[10]

There's a haze of cigarette smoke beneath the chandelier. The smell of the assembled company has grown stronger—there's a dryness and sweetness in the air, thick and exciting, a broth rich in ingredients, which for every person, but particularly for one who in his youth found it hard to get over an excessive sensitivity, brings back memories of a youthful broken heart... The Little Ones are still on the dance floor; since they love the party so much they are allowed to join in until eight o'clock. The young people have actually got used to them being there; and they have their own way of belonging to it. Actually they've split up; Beißer in his little blue velvet tunic is turning circles alone in the middle of the carpet, while Lorchen is having fun running after a dancing couple and trying to grab hold of the man by his dinner jacket. It's Max Hergesell with his lady, the Plaichinger girl. They move well, it's a pleasure to watch them. It has to be conceded that something joyful can be made out of these dances of the new, wild times if the right people take them up. Young Hergesell steps out superbly, following the rules but totally uninhibited by them, it seems. How elegantly he sweeps backwards, when there's space! But then also when there isn't, when there's a squeeze, he has a tasteful way of holding back, with the support of his agile partner, who comes up with the astonishing gracefulness of which well-built women are sometimes capable. They are chatting cheek to cheek and seem unaware of Lorchen following them. Some people are laughing at the little girl's persistence and, as the group sweeps past him, Doctor Cornelius tries to catch hold of his daughter and pull her towards him. But Lorchen evades him, seemingly in horror, and wants nothing to do with Abel at this moment. She doesn't recognize him, pushes her tiny arm against his chest and, with her dear little face turned away, anxious and troubled, struggles to get away from him and follow her whim.

The professor can't help feeling hurt. In this moment he hates the party, the stuff of which has confused the senses of his darling and torn her away from him. This love of his, which is not entirely free of mixed motives, not quite irreproachable in its roots, is vulnerable. He smiles mechanically, but his eyes have clouded over and have now fixed themselves on the pattern in the carpet, somewhere beneath the feet of the dancers.

'The little ones should go to bed,' he tells his wife. But she begs for another quarter of an hour for the children. They've been promised it because they've so enjoyed the hurly-burly. He smiles again and shakes his head, stays standing there for a moment and then goes to the cloakroom, which is overflowing with coats, scarves, hats and outdoor shoes.

He has trouble digging his own things out of the chaos, and then Max Hergesell comes to the cloakroom mopping his brow with a handkerchief.

'Herr Professor,' he says in the tone of all the Hergesells and with a young man's deference, 'are you going out? That's such a bind with my dancing shoes. They press like Charles the Great. They're just too small for me, I realize now, and that's quite apart from the stiffness of the leather. They're pressing here on the nail of my big toe,' he says, and stands on one leg while he holds the other foot in two hands. 'So I can say it bluntly. I've decided I must change them, my outdoor shoes will have to serve… oh, but let me help you!'

'Thank you but no,' says Cornelius. 'It's very kind of you but I can manage. You'd do better to relieve your own problem.' For Hergesell has got to his knees and has begun fastening the hooks and eyelets of Cornelius's boots.

The professor offers thanks, pleasantly touched by such a sincere and respectful readiness to offer him service. 'I wish you the continuation of a lovely evening, when you've changed your shoes. You really shouldn't dance in shoes that pinch. You really must swap them. Now goodbye, I must get some air.'

'I'll be dancing with Lorchen again in a moment!' Hergesell calls after him. 'She'll be a first-rate dancer when she's older. Guaranteed!'

'Do you think so?' Cornelius answers from the doorway. 'Yes, you're the expert and the champion. Just mind your back when you bend. You don't want to injure your spine.'

He winks and goes on his way. Nice lad, he thinks, as he puts distance between them. A university student of engineering, with a clear sense of purpose, everything sorted out. At the same time so friendly and good-looking. And his fatherly envy grabs hold of him again, because of his 'poor Bert', this feeling of uncertainty that puts the existence of the young man from outside in such a rosy light but makes that of his own son look terribly dim. With that thought he starts out on his evening walk.

He goes up the road, over the bridge and up the river on the far side, along the riverside walk as far as the next bridge but one. It's cold and wet and from time to time flecks of snow fall. He's turned up his collar, he's holding his walking stick pointing backwards, with the handle hooked over his arm, and every now and again he takes a deep breath of the winter evening air to ventilate his lungs. As usual when he is out for his constitutional, he thinks of his professional work, his lecture, the sentences that he will deliver tomorrow with regard to Philip's struggle against the German uprising, and which he hopes will be steeped in melancholy and do the subject justice. Do it justice above all! he thinks. Justice to the truth is the spirit of scholarly research, the principle of knowledge and the light in which one is bound to show things to young people, as much for the sake of intellectual discipline as for personal and humane reasons; in order not to clash with them and indirectly to offend them in their political views, which naturally today are so terribly divided and contrarian, with issues so often flaring up it's easy to get caught up in the squabbling of one side or another, and it may in turn cause a scandal when one advocates for a particular view of history. But then it isn't even historical to take a particular side; the only way to be historical is to do justice to the question. That's certainly the case, exactly it and properly considered... To do a subject justice is not to bring to it youthful passion, nor cheerful, pious and well-meaning single-mindedness;[11] the right approach is melancholy. If by nature this doing justice to a question is melancholy, then that's because by nature it secretly sympathizes more with the melancholic party, the power in history that has no hope, than with the cheerful, pious and well-meaning contingent. In the end history consists of such sympathy. Would there be no doing justice to a question without it? So perhaps there isn't justice in the end? the professor asks himself, and is so deeply immersed in this thought that he has put his letters in the box at the next bridge but one, without registering the fact and is now starting to walk back. It's a disturbing thought with regard to scholarly truth that he's running through his mind, but it too is scholarship, it too makes demands on conscience and psychology and must be tackled dutifully and without prejudice, whether it's disturbing or not… With such fanciful preoccupations going through his head Doctor Cornelius returns home.

Xaver is standing in the front porch and seems to have been watching out for him.

'Herr Professor,' Xaver says with those thick lips, and flicks his hair back. 'You'd be needin' to go up summit smartish to Lorchen. There's summit wrong.'

'What's wrong?' a shocked Cornelius asks. 'Is she ill?'

'Na, she aint ill essatly,' Xaver replies. 'Is jus summit got to 'er and she carn stop cryin. Ballin' her eyes out, she be. Is cos of that bloke, him what danced wiv 'er, the one in the penguin suit, Herr Hergesell. Coun get 'er to leave the 'all, could we? No way, and she cryin' 'er eyes out. Summit got to 'er cruel and no mistake.'

'Nonsense,' said the professor, who's come in through the door and thrown his things into the cloakroom. He says nothing more, opens the glass door, which is covered in coats, into the dining hall they're using as a ballroom and, without according the partygoers a glance, goes over to the staircase to the right. He takes the stairs two at a time, crosses the upstairs hall and turns into a little corridor beyond it directly into the nursery, followed by Xaver, who stays and waits at the door.

In the nursery all the lights are still on. There's a row of pictures—a brightly coloured paper frieze—running all round the walls. There's a big cupboard full of a heap of toys, a rocking horse with lacquered red nostrils is resting his hoof on its swinging rockers, and more toys—a miniature trumpet, building blocks, train carriages—are strewn about the linoleum floor. The little children's beds, white, stand close to each other, Lorchen's right in the corner by the window and Beißer's just a step away, towards the middle of the room.

Beißer is asleep. As usual, with the help of Blue Anna, he's said his prayers in a resonant voice and then immediately gone to sleep, a stormy, red-tinged, glowing and so unbelievably deep sleep that if a cannonball were fired right beside him it wouldn't disturb him; his clenched fists, thrown back on the pillow, lie either side of his head, close by the ill-fitting little wig of his hair that is sticky and messy from his deep sleep.

Lorchen's bed is surrounded by women: besides Blue Anna both the Hinterhöfer ladies are standing at the bedhead and discussing matters with her and among themselves. They step aside as the professor approaches, and he can see Lorchen sitting up there on her little pillow, pale and so bitterly crying and sobbing that Doctor Cornelius doesn't remember ever having seen her like that. Her beautiful child's hands are lying in front of her on the coverlet, her little nightdress with its narrow border of lace has slipped from one of her pathetically thin shoulders, and her head, this tiny sweet head that Cornelius loves so much because, thanks to the way the lower half of her face is more prominent, it sits so unexpectedly like a flower on top of the slender stem of her little girl's neck—she's thrown back her head, so that her tear-filled eyes are staring up at the corner where the wall and the ceiling meet, and there it appears that she continuously nods to the great pain in her heart; for, whether it is deliberate and a way of expressing herself, or because the sobbing has shattered her, her weeny little head just keeps nodding and wobbling, her quick-fire mouth meanwhile, with the upper lip shaped like a bow, is half-open, like a tiny mater dolorosa, and while the tears stream from her eyes she emits monotone sounds which have nothing to do with the angry and superfluous shrieks of naughty children but stem from real heartbreak and arouse in the professor, who as a rule cannot bear to see Lorchen cry and has never seen her cry like this, an unbearable pity.

It makes him sharp and snappy with the hovering Hinterhöfer women.

'There must be a lot of things that need doing with the supper,' he says in a state. 'I think we can leave it to the lady of the house to look after things here.'

Enough said for the sensitive ears of those who once belonged to the middle classes. Offended to the marrow, they remove themselves, mimicked and despised at the door by Xaver Kleinsgütl, who right from the start, no question about it, was born into the lower class and always enjoys making fun of the women who have fallen to his level.

'Darling, little one,' says Cornelius, choking, and grasps sad little Lorchen in his arms as he lowers himself on to the chair beside the little metal bed. 'What's wrong with my little girl?'

Her tears leave his face wet.

'Abel… Abel…' she stammers, sobbing, 'Why… is… Max… not my brother? Max… has… to be my brother…'

What a misfortune, what a terrible misfortune! What has the infernal dance party gone and done, thinks Cornelius, and, completely at a loss as to what to do, he looks up at Blue Anna, who is standing there quietly and proudly, conscious of her position, with her hands folded against her apron at the end of the bed.

'It's because of the fact,' she says severely and knowingly, with her lower lip drawn tight, 'that the womanly instincts manifest themselves with such extraordinary intensity in this child.'

'Hold your tongue, woman,' replies Cornelius in torment. He tells himself he should be glad at least that Lorchen has not withdrawn from him, she's not pushing him away like she did just now on the dance floor but cuddling up to him and looking for help, while she repeats her stupid, confused wish that Max should be her brother and plangently demands to go back to him, on the dance floor, so that he can dance with her again. But Max is on the dance floor with Fräulein Plaichinger, who is a full-grown colossus and has all the rights to him—while Lorchen has never before struck the professor, who is so torn apart by pity, as so tiny and sparrow-like as now, when, helpless and wracked with sobs, she cuddles up to him and doesn't know what things are happening to her poor little soul. She doesn't know. It's not clear to her that she's suffering because of the plump, fully grown, fully entitled Plaichinger, who is allowed to take to the dance floor with Max Hergesell, while Lorchen was only allowed to do it once in fun, as a joke, although she is incomparably more worthy of love. On the other hand, to reproach young Hergesell on those grounds would be quite impossible, because it would amount to a crazy imposition on him. Lorchen's pain is lawless and desperate, and any pain like that would have to conceal itself. But because it's unreasonable its expression is also uninhibited, and that creates a great embarrassment. It's nothing at all to Blue Anna and Xaver, they're not sensitive to it, whether it's because they're stupid or just dully inclined to see nature taking its course. But in Cornelius the heart of a father is totally distraught at the embarrassment, as well as riven by the shock and the shame of a lawless and desperate passion.

It doesn't help for him to explain to poor Lorchen that she has an excellent little brother in the person of Beißer, soundly asleep alongside her. Through her tears all she does, as one who is suffering, is cast a look of contempt towards the other bed and ask for Max. Nor does it help that he promises her they can do an extra-long five-man walk tomorrow in the dining room and paints a picture in glowing detail of how they will play the cushion game at the table. She doesn't want to know about any of that, nor lie down and go to sleep. She doesn't want to sleep, she wants to sit up and suffer... But then they, Abel and Lorchen, both detect the sound of something miraculous just now happening, step by step, two sets of feet taking two steps each, as it approaches the nursery and overwhelmingly manifests itself...

It's Xaver's doing—that's immediately clear. Xaver Kleinsgütl wasn't standing the whole time beside the door where he poured scorn on the ladies who had fallen from their social class. He had woken up to the situation, decided on a course of action and made the arrangements. He had gone down to the ballroom, taken Herr Hergesell by the arm, said something to him with his thick lips and asked him if he would be so kind. Here they are now, both of them. Xaver once again stays by the door, having played his part; but Max Hergesell enters the room and crosses to Lorchen's iron bedstead, in his dinner jacket and with the start of a dark beard showing through beside his ears and his fine black eyes—he arrives evidently in total conviction of his role as a bringer of happiness, fairy-tale prince and knight in the guise of a swan, as one who says: what's all this then, here I am, nothing more to worry about!

Cornelius is as overwhelmed as Lorchen.

'Just look who's come!' he says weakly. 'That's extremely kind of Herr Hergesell.'

'Not at all, nothing out of the ordinary,' says Hergesell. 'It's a perfectly normal thing that a man should check on his dancing partner again and wish her goodnight.'

And he goes up to the bedstead where Lorchen is sitting in silence. She smiles blissfully through her tears. A high little sound, something approaching a sob of happiness, further escapes her lips, and then she stares up at her knight with her golden eyes which, although they are red and swollen, are so incomparably more lovely than those of the burly Plaichinger girl. She doesn't lift her little arms to hug him. Her happiness is no more intelligible to her than her pain, but she doesn't do it. Her beautiful little hands with the blue veins remain still on the coverlet, while Max Hergesell rests his arms on the bed rail as if on the railings of a balcony.

'The hope is that she won't sit crying on her bed in night after night of distress!' he says, and casts a glance at the professor, fishing for approval for his learning.[12] 'Hah, at such an age! "Rest easy, my lovely child!"[13] You are good. You can become something. You just need to stay as you are. Hah, at such an age! Lollipolly, now that I'm here will you not stop crying and go to sleep?'

Lorchen looks at him transfigured. Her skinny shoulders are bare; the professor pulls up the sheet with the lace border to cover them; it makes him think of a sentimental story about a dying child who is visited by a clown he has watched with such stupendous joy at the circus. He comes to the child on his deathbed wearing his costume with silver butterflies embroidered front and back, and the child dies happy. Max Hergesell is not in fancy dress, and Lorchen is not about to die, for heaven's sake, it's just that 'it really got to her'; but otherwise there is a similarity with the story, and the feelings inspired in the professor towards young Hergesell, who is leaning there and coming out with daft things—more for the father than for the child, but Lorchen doesn't notice—are a thoroughly weird mixture of gratitude, embarrassment, hatred and admiration.

'Goodnight, Lollipolly,' Hergesell says, and reaches his hand through the rail. Her beautiful tiny white hand vanishes in his big strong red one. 'Sleep well! Sweet dreams! But not about me! For heaven's sake not! At that age! Ha!' And so he ends his fairy-tale clown visit, accompanied by Cornelius to the door.

'Nothing to thank me for! Don't mention it!' he insists politely and generously while they walk; and Xaver joins him to go down and serve the Italian salad.

But Doctor Cornelius turns back to Lorchen, who is now lying down with her cheek on her flat little pillow.

'That was nice,' he says, while he tenderly arranges the coverlet around her, and she nods with a deep breath mingled with a sob that catches in her throat. He sits a good quarter of an hour by her bed and watches her fall asleep, following her little brother, who took the right path so much earlier. Her beautiful silky brown hair falls in curls as it usually does when she's asleep; her long eyelashes close tightly over those eyes that have wept so many tears; her angelic mouth with the curving, bow-shaped upper lip stands open in sweet satisfaction, and only now and again does a late, stray sob disturb her slow breathing.

And her little hands, pinkish-white little hands like blossoms, how they lie there, one on the blue of the eiderdown, the other in front of her face on the pillow! Doctor Cornelius's heart fills with tenderness like wine.

What good fortune, he thinks, that with every breath of this slumber Lethe streams into her little soul; that the night of a child, from one day to the next, should reveal such a deep and wide abyss! Tomorrow it's certain that young Hergesell will be no more than a pale shadow, without the power to intrude on her heart and in happy oblivion she will join Abel and Beißer in abandoning herself to the five-man walk and the thrilling game with the cushion.

Thank heaven for that!

(1925)

MARIO AND
THE MAGICIAN
A Tragic Holiday Memory

IT WAS THE ATMOSPHERE in Torre di Venere that makes recalling that holiday so unpleasant. From the beginning there was anger, irritation and tension in the air, and then at the end came the shock of that terrible Cipolla, who seemed in his very person to embody the menace in the air and intensify it. He left a stark impression in human terms as one who embodied something fateful. That, terrifyingly, the children were present at the end was an aberration in itself. It rested on a dismal misunderstanding. (That end lay in the nature of things and we should have foreseen it, though it only struck us afterwards.) The false ways in which that eccentric creature presented himself were to blame. Thank goodness the children didn't understand where theatre ended and catastrophe began, and we left them happy in the illusion that it had all been part of the show.

Torre lies about fifteen kilometres from Portoclemente, one of the most popular summer resorts on the Tyrrhenian Sea. It's an elegant town, chock-a-block with visitors from one month to the next, with its lively street of hotels and markets leading down to the sea, its broad beach covered in beach huts, sandcastles with flags atop, brown human bodies and noisy entertainments. Since the beach, with pine woods running alongside, and mountains right up close and looking down on it, and since this whole coast boasts a very inviting and untouched expanse of fine sand, it's no surprise that rival resorts should have quietly set themselves up a bit further along: Torre di Venere, a place by the way where you will search in vain for the long since disappeared tower that gives it its name, is as a holiday destination an outlier of its grander neighbour and was for a few years a refuge for the elite, an idyllic spot for those who liked its undeveloped quality. However, as usually happens with such places, those in search of peace had to move further on some time ago, in the direction of Marina Petriera and who knows where; everyone grasps how it is, the world has only to pounce with comic enthusiasm on a quiet, untouched place than those qualities are destroyed. It has this mad idea it can partner with peace and quiet; be part of them without spoiling them; it can set up a whole industry of noise and fun in their place and still believe peace and quiet have not been lost. That's how Torre, while still more tranquil and more modest than Portoclemente, has become much sought-after by Italians and foreigners. It's no longer the fashion to go to the world-famous holiday destination, even if it's the case that nothing changes and it's still a noisy, oversubscribed resort of world renown. No, the fashion is to go next door, to Torre, a more refined place, they think, and cheaper too; and these factors go on being attractions, even though they're no longer true. Torre has now got its own Grand Hotel; numerous pensions from the sophisticated to the simple have popped up; the owners and tenants of summer houses in the pine-dune gardens above the sea are no longer the only people on the beach below; in July and August the picture is no different from that in Portoclemente; you can't move for clamouring, querulous, excited holidaymakers in full throat, getting burnt on the back of the neck by a merciless hot sun shining down; children are at the helm of flat-bottomed, brightly coloured boats, rocking on the dazzling blue of the sea, and the air is full of their resonant names as their mothers lose them out of sight and start to worry, while vendors tread carefully over the prostrated limbs of the sunbathers, offering them, in the typical gravelly, unrestrained voices of the south, oysters, drinks, flowers, coral jewellery and *cornetti al burro*—the best croissants, made with butter.

That's what the beach in Torre looked like when we arrived—pretty enough, but we had the sense nevertheless that we'd come too early. It was the middle of August, the Italian season was still in full flow; that's not the right moment for foreigners to appreciate the charm of a place. What a crowd there was in the afternoons, in the outdoor cafés along the promenade beside the beach, like the Esquisito, where we sometimes sat and were served by Mario, the same Mario whose story I'm about to tell! You could hardly find a table, and the various bands, though they pretended the others didn't exist, all played together in a crazy cacophony. And then in the afternoons people also arrive from Portoclemente, swelling the numbers; for of course Torre is a popular destination for guests from that other resort looking for something to do, and, thanks to the Fiat cars tearing back and forth, the laurels and oleanders all along the edge of the main road linking the two places are plastered inches thick in white dust—quite a sight, but not a pleasant one.

Really, one should go to Torre di Venere in September, when the vast majority of people have left, or in May, before the sea has reached a temperature that will tempt people living in the south to dip a toe in. Nor is it empty in the early and late seasons either, but the atmosphere is more moderate and less dominated by the home nation. You hear mainly English, French and German on the shaded verandas of the beach huts and in the pension dining rooms, whereas in August, at least in the Grand Hotel, where, for want of something more intimate, we had booked rooms, you can find yourself so much at the mercy of a clientele from Florence and Rome as to feel isolated and treated as a second-class guest.

This was our rather annoying experience on the evening of our arrival, when we turned up in the dining room and a waiter on duty there showed us to a table. There was nothing wrong with that table, but we couldn't help noticing the adjacent glass-walled terrace looking out to sea, which was as busy as the dining room but had the odd free table, and on top of that all the tables were lit with little red-shaded lamps. Our children were very taken with the sight, and so we said we'd rather have our meal out there—a venture that proved our ignorance, as it turned out, for it was made plain to us, with some embarrassment, that that alluring place to sit was reserved for 'our clients'—*ai nostri clienti*. For our clients? But that was us. We weren't just passing by, we weren't day-trippers, but for three or four weeks we belonged there, as guests, paying for our meals. But then we let it go. We didn't insist on knowing what distinguished people like us from those clients permitted to eat beneath the red glow of the little lamps, and we ate our *pranzo* at an ordinary, prosaic table in the middle of the room, lit by a ceiling light. But I must say it was very mediocre fare, just the sort of routine stuff they serve in hotels, with no character and very little taste; subsequently we found the cooking in the Pensione Eleonora, just ten paces away from the sea, very much better.

In fact we moved over there before we even got settled in the Grand Hotel, after three or four days—not because of the terrace and the pretty lamps; the children, who had immediately made friends with a variety of waiters and bellboys, were so delighted with the sea that they soon lost all thought of those enticing coloured lights. But there arose with certain terrace clients, or, more specifically, with the hotel management, and them alone, because of the way they crawled to them, the kind of conflict that could leave an awkward stamp on a holiday right from the beginning. The terrace clients included top Roman aristocracy, a Principe X with his family, and because the room belonging to these guests was close to ours, the princess, at once a grand lady and a passionate mother, had become alarmed at the tail-end of an attack of whooping cough that our little ones had both recently recovered from, and which now and again still interrupted the otherwise rock-solid sleep of the younger one. The nature of this disease is not well known to science, leaving plenty of room here for superstitious beliefs, so we didn't ever hold it against the princess that she subscribed to the widely held view that whooping cough was acoustically infectious and feared it would set a bad example for her children. A woman who felt that she could be nothing but right, she sailed up to the management, and they, in the person of the figure in the frock coat who ran the hotel, whose acquaintance we had already made, hastened to let us know, with great regret, that in the circumstances it was an unavoidable necessity for us to move out of the main building into the hotel annexe. To insist that this childhood illness was in its last stages and should be considered over and posed no danger to others around was in vain. All that was conceded was that the case had been brought before the medical council and the hotel doctor—and he alone, not for instance a doctor we might have consulted—would be asked to make a decision. We agreed to this procedure, convinced that it would at once pacify the princess and avoid for us the nuisance of moving. So the doctor arrives and proves himself to be a decent and loyal servant of his profession. He examines the boy, pronounces him fully recovered and refutes any worries to the contrary. We're already feeling that the problem is over when the manager declares that we must vacate our room and move to the annexe, whatever the doctor has to say.

This byzantine reasoning outraged us. It's unlikely that the incredible stubbornness we ran up against came from the princess. The servile manager had probably not even dared to let her know what the doctor's verdict was. In any case we gave him notice as of that moment that we preferred to leave the hotel entirely and to do so immediately, and went off to pack. We could do that with a light heart because in the meantime we'd been in contact with the Pensione Eleonora, whose inviting external appearance had made such a good impression on us, and met its owner, Signora Angiolieri, whom we found to be a very sympathetic person. Mrs Angiolieri, a slight woman with dark eyes, a Tuscan type, probably in her early thirties, with the matt-ivory complexion of women from the south, and her husband, a painstakingly dressed, quiet, bald man, owned a bigger guesthouse in Florence and only came to manage the branch in Torre di Venere in summer and early autumn. Before she got married, though, our new landlady had been a helpmeet, travelling companion and wardrobe manager, as well as a friend, to the great Eleonora Duse, a period of her life that she obviously regarded as the happiest, and right from our arrival she immediately began to tell us all about it in vivid detail. Umpteen photographs of the great actress, with friendly dedications, and also other souvenirs from that time together adorned the tables and shelves in Mrs Angiolieri's sitting room, and although it was obvious that she was using the cult of her interesting past to increase the attraction of her present enterprise, we were happy to listen, and found it all very interesting as she led us through the house, talking staccato in her melodious Tuscan voice of how instinctively kind her former employer had been, how deftly she could sympathize with others, a woman with a real genius of the heart who would never be forgotten.

So we had our things brought there, to the sorrow of the staff at the Grand Hotel who had such a typical Italian love of children. The room we moved into was pleasant and quiet, within easy reach of the sea, along an avenue of young plane trees that ran down to the promenade. The dining room, where every lunchtime Mrs Angiolieri herself served the soup, was cool and clean, the service pleasant and attentive, the catering superb, and we even ran into some people we knew from Vienna, and after dinner we sat outside chatting, and through them we met more new people, and so everything might have turned out well. We were thoroughly satisfied with our move, and nothing stood in the way of a perfect holiday.

And yet we never had the chance to settle. Perhaps, nevertheless, something lingered from the stupid cause of our change of hotel—I'm willing to admit that personally I really don't like that kind of clash with clannish local ways—the naïve misuse of power, the unfairness, the simpering corruption. I can't get that sort of thing out of my head, I keep finding myself irritated thinking about it, and it's completely unproductive because such behaviour is massively taken for granted and seen as natural. At the same time, we hadn't finished with the Grand Hotel. The children kept up their friendships there as before, one of the porters mended their toys, and now and again we drank tea in the garden, not without catching sight of the princess who, with her lips painted coral-red, appeared with mincing steps to see where her darlings had got to with their English nanny and didn't notice our suspect presence in the vicinity, for as soon as we spotted her we forbade our boy even to clear his throat.

The heat was overwhelming, should I add that? It was African; the tyrannical rule of the sun, the moment one left the freshness of the indigo-blue water's edge, was so unremitting that just the few steps from the beach to the lunch table, wearing only the loosest clothes, confronted us with an exhausting challenge. Do you like that? Do you like it for weeks on end? It's true it's the south, it's the weather of the classical world, the climate of that great flowering of human culture, Homer's sun, and so on. But after a while, I can't help it, I can easily come to feel that it's oppressive. It makes me apathetic. The overheated emptiness of the sky day after day becomes a burden, the sharpness of the colours, the monstrous naivety of the uninterrupted light does indeed make you feel you're on holiday; you feel carefree and there are no whimsical changes of weather to upset your plans; but without our perhaps fully taking it in at the beginning, this climate frustrates the deeper, far from simple needs of the northern soul and creates a kind of desert within, and with time encourages something like contempt. You're right, without that really stupid fuss over the whooping cough I probably wouldn't have felt it this way; I was on edge, that was what I wanted to feel, and half unconsciously I was looking around for a rational motive, if not to bring that feeling about but then to legitimate and strengthen it. Our disgruntlement played a role. You have to take that into account. When you think of the sea, and of a morning spent sitting on the fine sand beside it, in all its infinite splendour, it's impossible to harbour negative thoughts of that kind, and yet it was the case that despite all our previous experience we didn't feel easy on the beach; we weren't happy.

We'd come too early in the year, it was still in the hands of the local middle class. They were very good to look at as human types, and, you're right, among the young people there were many well-behaved, gracious and charming human beings. But inevitably all around them was human mediocrity and social scum, which, you must admit, is no more attractive in this part of the world than back home with us. The *voices* these women have! Now and again you can hardly believe you're in the birthplace of the Western art-song. 'Fuggièro!' I can still hear that name being shouted in my ear, having heard it twenty days on end a hundred times emanating from right beside me, gravelly, raucous, insistently ugly, with a coarse open 'è', uttered with some kind of desperation that had become mechanical. 'Fuggièro! Come 'ere when you're called!' Whereupon the vulgarity became yet another irritation in itself for someone in such a bad mood as I was. The shrieking was aimed at a revolting boy with a disgusting patch of sunburn between his shoulders—a boy who in my experience set a new record for being nasty, coarse and uncouth, and who on top of that was a great coward, capable, with the huge self-pitying fuss he was making, of upsetting the whole beach. One day there had been an incident when a crab had pinched one of his toes in the water, and the cry he let out, like a classical hero in pain, on the occasion of this minuscule discomfort, shocked me to the core and made me think something terrible had happened. Evidently he felt he'd been seriously poisoned. Crawling on to the sand, he threw himself about in apparently unbearable pain, shouting and groaning, Ooh, ooh, alas, alack, and he hit out with his arms and legs, rejecting the tragic imprecations of his mother and the sympathy of others further off. People ran up from all sides. A doctor was called, the same man who had dealt with our whooping cough issue so professionally, and once again he showed his sober expertise. He offered his kindly sympathy but said it was nothing at all and recommended simply that the patient go back into the sea, to cool down the tiny nip in his toe. Instead of that, though, Fuggièro was carried from the beach on an improvised stretcher, like a fallen hero, or a victim of drowning, all that only to return the next morning and, pretending not to notice what he was doing, to destroy other children's sandcastles. In a word the boy was an outrage.

Meanwhile let it be said that this twelve-year-old was one of the main bearers of a public mood that, though it was hard to put a name to, turned our lovely holiday into something unbearable. The prevailing attitude somehow lacked innocence; it was uneasy; local people like those around Fuggièro on the beach were strutting about, pleased with themselves—one couldn't quite fathom what was meant, why were they parading their dignity, making a show of their seriousness and their strength and their sense of honour, their alertness, in front of foreigners and each other? What was it about? And then one realized that it was about politics, and that it was the idea of the nation that had set certain things in motion. Indeed the whole beach was rife with patriotic children—an unnatural and depressing experience. I mean children are a human species and a society of their own, they are, as it were, their own nation; they are very easily driven to find themselves a life in common, even with few words, expressed in different languages. Ours too played just as often with children from elsewhere as from back home. But we could see they experienced some puzzling setbacks. There were tricky moments, expressions of self-assertion that seemed to be too awkward and formulaic to have anything much to do with selfhood, a quarrel over flags, a dispute over who was the leader and who was the best; grown-ups intervened not so much to mediate as to take a decisive step and establish some principles, there was talk of the greatness and the dignity of Italy, talk that wasn't well meant and was spoiling the games; we noticed our two taken aback and not knowing what to do, walk away, and it was difficult for us to explain the situation to them somehow or other: these people, we said, were going through a state of affairs rather like an illness, they could think of it like that, and it wasn't very pleasant but apparently it had to happen.

It was our fault, we had to blame our own lack of caution, that we now came into conflict with a situation which we had ourselves recognized and tried to dignify with an explanation—I mean we got into yet another conflict, for it appeared that what had gone on before was not a matter of entirely unconnected coincidences. Briefly, we were offending the official morality. Our little daughter, eight years old, but who in terms of her bodily development might easily be taken for a year younger, since she was as skinny as a rake, had been swimming in the sea for a long time, given that it was so warm, and when she came out and went back to playing in the sand in her wet costume, we allowed her to take the costume that was by now thickly covered in sand and wash it in the sea, with the idea that she would put it back on and take care not to get in such a mess again. So she runs naked the few metres to the water's edge, dips her swimsuit in the sea and comes back. Could we have foreseen the wave of contempt, disapproval and protest that her behaviour, that is, our behaviour, awakened? I'm not here to deliver a lecture, but in the last decade across the whole world the attitude to the body and to nakedness has fundamentally changed, and thus the way people feel about it. There are some things that one 'doesn't think twice about' and to them belonged the freedom that we had afforded to this child's body, which really should have caught no one's eye. Yet around here they made a huge fuss about it. The patriotic children jeered, Fuggièro whistled through his fingers. Everywhere in our vicinity the adults were talking excitedly, loud enough for us to hear, and it didn't bode well. A fellow dressed for the town, a really flashy type, wearing, pushed to the back of his head, a bowler hat that was hardly suited to the beach, is at that very moment reassuring his outraged ladies that he will take steps to put the situation right, and we are buried under the philippic he launches, a diatribe that takes all the southern love of the sensual life and turns it into a prim assertion of discipline and public decency. The shamelessness of our actions, he said, was all the more worthy of condemnation insofar as it amounted to an ungrateful and offensive abuse of Italian hospitality. It was not only that the spirit and the letter of public bathing regulations had been flouted, but the honour of his country impugned, and in his concern to uphold that honour he, the townie in the flashy suit, would make sure that our insult to the dignity of the nation would not go unnoticed.

We did our best to heed this suasion, punctuating it with nods of the head. To rebut the overheated fellow would undoubtedly have meant falling from one error into the next. We had things on the tip of our tongue, for instance, that the complexity of the situation meant that the word 'hospitality' in the strictest sense was somewhat out of place, and that it was no euphemism to say we were not only Italy's guests but Signora Angiolieri's, who as of a few years back had exchanged a post as companion to Eleonora Duse to enter the hotel business. We were also tempted to retort that we hadn't realized that moral turpitude in this lovely country had ever reached such a degree that a reaction in terms of prudishness and hypersensitivity might seem understandable and even necessary. But we restricted ourselves to assuring the fellow that we had had no intention to provoke anyone or show disrespect and, justifying ourselves with reference to her tender age, we suggested that our young delinquent had hardly committed a grave offence. All in vain. Our assurances were rejected as unconvincing, our defence found to be pathetic, and it would be necessary to make an example of us. I think someone must have contacted the authorities by telephone, whereupon their

representative appeared on the beach, called the case a very serious one, *molto grave*, and we had to follow him up to the square,
to the town hall, the *municipio*, where someone higher up likewise
pronounced the provisional verdict '*molto grave*', expatiated about
our actions in exactly the same streetwise, didactic terminology as
the man in the rigid hat, and for our sins fined us the sum of fifty
lire. We considered this contribution to Italy's domestic economy
well worth the adventure it brought us. We paid and walked off.
Ought we to have left altogether that moment?

Indeed we should have done. In that case we could have avoided
the fateful Cipolla; but then a lot of other things came together
that made us put off changing the location of our holiday. A poet
has said it's torpor that binds us to painful situations—maybe that
aperçu goes some way to explaining our stubbornness. It's also
the case that when something like that happens one doesn't feel
like giving way; one hesitates to admit having created an impossible situation, and the occasional expression of sympathy makes
one feel all the more defiant. In the Villa Eleonora just one voice
spoke up against the injustice of what had happened to us. Some
Italians we'd met after dinner told us they thought it did nothing
for the reputation of the country, and announced the intention
of having a word with the fellow in the flashy suit, as one Italian
to another. But he was gone from the beach the next day, along
with his group—not because of us, of course, but perhaps because
awareness of his imminent departure had helped put him up to
the deed; and anyway his absence made things easier for us. Not
to put too fine a point on it, we stayed also because our visit had
become interesting to us, and because being interesting has a
value in itself, distinct from any pleasure or displeasure. Should
one set sail, and avoid something that suddenly looks as if it may
not go well? Should one 'pack one's bags' when life turns a bit

strange, when things seem not quite in order and are likely to cause awkwardness and offence? Of course not, resoundingly no, one ought to stay and see what happens and perhaps learn something from one's exposure to the turn of events. So we stayed put and the terrible reward for our resoluteness was the unholy appearance of Cipolla.

I haven't mentioned that we were fined by the state for our infraction just as the high season was coming to an end. Our severe friend in his rigid hat, the flashy townie, was not the only visitor to leave the resort; there was quite an exodus, you could see all the luggage carts heading in the direction of the station. The beach divested itself of its national clientele, life in Torre, in the cafés, on the paths through the pine trees and past the summer houses became less crowded and more European; and probably now we could even have eaten on the glass-walled terrace of the Grand Hotel, but we had no inclination to do that, we were perfectly fine with Signora Angiolieri—perfectly fine to be understood in a shade of meaning relative to the general daemonic spirit of the place. But at the same time as this welcome and beneficial change came about, the weather also turned. It showed itself to be in tune almost to the hour with when most people chose to take their holidays. The sky became overcast, and, though it didn't get any cooler, the inferno we'd been enduring for the eighteen days since our arrival (and which must have been in place long before that) gave way to the sticky, airless days of the scirocco, and from time to time a light rain spattered across the velvety sand where we spent our mornings. Another thing too: we'd already spent two-thirds of our intended time in Torre; yet the deflated, colour-less sea, awash with torpid jellyfish in its shallows, was a novelty, and it would have been foolish to want the sun back, after all the endurance its excessive reign had required.

And this was the moment when Cipolla turned up. Maestro Cipolla, as they called him on the posters, which one day suddenly went up everywhere, including in the dining room of the Pensione Eleonora. A travelling virtuoso, a master entertainer, *forzatore*, *illusionista* and *prestidigiatore* (as he styled himself), this circus strongman, illusionist and conjuror was about to present before the revered public of Torre di Venere some extraordinary and mysterious tricks that would endlessly puzzle them. A master of the art of magic! The advertisement alone was enough to turn our children's heads. They'd never been to a magic show before, and this holiday should afford them that new thrill. For hours they kept on at us to buy tickets for an evening with the master of spells, and although the late hour of the occasion, nine o'clock, already gave us pause, we weighed up the possibility that we would probably go home after we'd seen a few examples of Cipolla's probably modest art, that the children could anyway sleep it off in the morning, and acquired from Signora Angiolieri herself, who had some good seats to hand, on commission, for her guests, our four tickets. She couldn't swear to the quality of the performance, and we weren't reckoning with that either; but even we felt the need for some diversion, and the impatient curiosity of the children had a kind of infectiousness about it.

The place where the maestro was to perform was a public amenity which during the high season served as a cinema with a programme changing every week. We'd never been there. To get there one had to go past the '*palazzo*', a crumbling castle wall dating from feudal times that was incidentally for sale, and follow the main road, where there were also a chemist's, a hairdresser's, all the most useful shops, and which led as it were from the feudal era through the bourgeois and into the age of the people; for it ran from poor fishermen's cottages, where old women were sitting outside the doors mending nets, to this spot, beloved of the petty bourgeoisie, where the '*sala*' stood, in fact not much more than a covered wooden stage, spacious, it was true, with, to either side, brightly coloured posters stuck over each other. In between was an arch that served as the entrance. And so, some time after dinner on the agreed day, we made our pilgrimage there in the dark, the children in their best clothes, a dress for her, a suit for him, enchanted by the special occasion. It was warm and humid, as it had been for days, there was the occasional flash of lightning and a few bursts of rain. We carried umbrellas. It was a quarter of an hour on foot.

We showed our tickets as we entered and then we had to find our seats. They were in the third row on the left, and as we sat down we couldn't help noticing that the notion of a starting time for the performance, late enough as it was, was very vague; the audience, which seemed to make a point of coming late, took an age to fill up the stalls, which, since there were no side rows, was the extent of the auditorium. This tardiness was something of a concern for us. The children already had red cheeks from a hectic mixture of expectation and tiredness. Only the standing places in the side aisles and at the back were already full when we arrived. There they stood, the varied indigenous male population of Torre di Venere, with their bare arms folded on striped jerseys, fisher-men among them, and young lads on the lookout for something to happen; and while we had no objection in the least to the pres-ence of this popular local element, which always brings colour and humour to an occasion like this, the children were absolutely delighted. For they had friends in this crowd, acquaintances they had made on afternoon walks to beaches further afield. Often, about the time the sun, exhausted by its tremendous day's work, was sinking into the sea and turning the tips of the waves red-gold as the tide advanced, we would come across, on our way home, groups of fishermen standing bare-legged in a row as, with a vocal heave-ho, they raised their arms and drew in their nets, transferring their catch of the day, usually not much, into dripping baskets; and the little ones watched them, directing their fragments of Italian at this or that man; they helped with the ropes and became firm friends. Now they were exchanging greetings with people in the standing audience. There was Guiscardo, there was Antonio, they knew their names and whispered them out loud with a wave in that direction, receiving in exchange a nod of the head or a smile of very fine teeth. Look, look, there's Mario from the Esquisito, Mario who brings us our hot chocolate! He wants to see the magician too, and he must have come early, because he's almost right in the front, but he doesn't notice us, he's not paying attention, that's his way, despite the fact that he's a waiter. So we turn our attention to the man who rents out the paddle boats on the shore who's also standing there, right at the back.

It turned a quarter past nine, almost half past nine. You can understand we were getting anxious; when would we get the children to bed? It had been a mistake to bring them here, for to expect them to break off their pleasure almost as soon as it had begun would be very hard. In time the stalls were almost full; the whole of Torre was there, one might say, the guests from the Grand Hotel, the guests from the Villa Eleonora and other pensions, and people we recognized from the beach. You could hear English and German. You could hear the French that Romanians, is it, speak with Italians. Madame Angiolieri herself was sitting two rows behind us beside her bald, silent husband, who was stroking his moustache with the two middle fingers of his right hand. Everyone arrived late but no one was too late; Cipolla kept his audience waiting.

149

He kept his audience waiting is, I'm sure, the right way to put it, for he increased the tension by delaying his appearance. People were sympathetic to this manoeuvre, although only up to a point. Around half past nine they began to clap—a nice enough way to show legitimate impatience since it also expresses the urge to applaud. For the children it was all part of the fun to join in. All children like clapping their appreciation. From the grass-roots section of the audience someone called out vigorously: '*Pronti!*' and '*Cominciamo!*' And lo and behold, just a shout of 'We're ready!', 'Let's get on with it!' and whatever hindrances had stood in the way for so long vanished and there was no difficulty beginning. There came the sound of a gong, to which people in the standing audience responded with a chorus of Ah!, and the curtain opened. It revealed a podium whose furnishings made it look more like a schoolroom than the place where a conjuror was about to show off his tricks, and that was because of the blackboard that stood on an easel in the left foreground. Otherwise there was an ordinary yellow coat-stand, a couple of straw-seated chairs in the local style and, further to the back of the stage, a small round table could be seen on which stood a bottle of water and a glass and, on a separate tray, a flask of some bright-yellow liquid with liqueur glasses alongside. There were just a couple of seconds in which to take in these props. Then, without the lights going down maestro Cipolla made his entrance.

He came in smartly, as if to show his devotion to the audience. He gave the false impression that he had been rushing, and not just now, but for a while back, to meet the crowd, whereas in truth he'd all the time just been standing in the wings. What he was wearing reinforced the fiction that he was coming from outside. A man whose age was hard to tell, but certainly not young, with a sharp, pockmarked face, piercing eyes, lines around his mouth and lips pressed together, a little black toothbrush moustache and a so-called goatee between his underlip and chin, he was dressed elegantly and elaborately as if out for an evening in town. He wore a broad, sleeveless black cloak with a velvet collar and satin-lined pelerine shoulders, which he held together with his arms fixed rather awkwardly in front of him. His hands were clad in white gloves, and a white scarf lay round his neck and a top hat with a curved brim was pulled down low over his brow. Much more than anywhere else, the eighteenth century is still alive and kicking in Italy, and along with it the character of the charlatan, the shameless clown who was so typical of that era and of whom one can still find quite good examples surviving in Italy. The whole way Cipolla was dressed owed a great deal to this historical model, and the impression of a boastful, fantastical buffoon, which was part of the picture, was awoken by the fact that his unusual, fancy clothes didn't quite fit, were somehow cut wrongly, pulling at the seams, and appeared not so much worn by his body as hung on it: there was something about his figure that wasn't right, neither from the front nor from behind—and later that became clearer. But I must emphasize that his manner, his face, his behaviour showed nothing of the clown, nothing that would suggest he was essentially a jester; rather more they spoke of a deep earnestness, the rejection of any attempt at humour, occasionally a rather nasty pride, and of the gloating of a cripple—although this didn't stop him in the beginning from inviting widespread laughter in the audience.

There was no more dear-public-at-your-service about him. The way he strode on to the stage turned out to be an expression of energy, with nothing subordinate about it. Standing there and tugging in leisurely fashion at the fingers of his gloves, he removed them to reveal long and yellowish hands, one of them wearing a signet ring adorned with a high-set lapis stone. His hard little eyes, with bags beneath them, took a long look at the audience, not hurrying, fastening here and there on a face he examined more closely, his lips held tight, not uttering a word. He rolled his gloves up in a ball and now threw them quite a distance, as if casually but with astonishing skill so that they landed right in the water glass on the little round table, and then, continuing to look around silently at the audience, produced a packet of cigarettes out of some inside pocket. You could see from the packet that they were the cheapest, state-produced variety you could buy. Pulling one out with his fingertips, and without looking what he was doing, he lit it with a petrol lighter. The lighter worked first time. He inhaled deeply and then, arrogantly grimacing, drawing his lips back, he puffed out a stream of grey smoke, all the while gently tapping his foot. His exposed teeth were sharp and uncared-for.

The public stared at him as intently as he did at them. The young people in the standing places could be seen with furrowed brows, giving him penetrating looks, waiting to see how this cocky fellow would begin his act. He gave no sign of anything of the kind. Getting out his packet of cigarettes and his lighter and then putting them back was awkward because of the clothes he was wearing; while he was doing so he loosened his cloak and one could see that on his left arm he had a leather loop from which hung, rather incongruously, a riding whip with a silver top like a claw. One could also see that he wasn't wearing evening dress but a frock coat, and as he loosened this too one caught sight of a the multicoloured sash that Cipolla wore close to his body, half-covered by his waistcoat. In a whispered exchange, the people sitting behind us took it to be the sign that the maestro had been honoured by his country (for the posters said he held the rank of *Cavaliere*). I'll leave that question open, since I've never heard that with the rank of *Cavaliere* goes any kind of ribbon like that. Perhaps the sash was pure humbug, just like the way this trickster was standing around, saying nothing, just taking his time and making a big thing of casually smoking a cigarette in front of his audience.

People laughed, as I said, and the good mood spread, even as a loud, dry voice in the standing places called out: '*Buona sera!*'

Cipolla heard it and sprang up. 'Who was that?' he asked, as if looking for a confrontation. 'Who spoke just now? Come on! First so cheeky and then afraid? *Paura*, huh?' He spoke with a rather high, somewhat asthmatic, metallic voice. He waited.

'It was me,' said a young man, breaking the silence, as if honoured at being singled out and rising to the challenge. He was a handsome lad, right near us, in a cotton shirt with his jacket hung over one shoulder. He had stiff black hair, thick as a brush, and he wore it standing up and untamed, as was the fashionable haircut in the newly awakened nation, and it made him look rather strange and African. '*Bè*—OK, so it was me. It ought to have been your job. But I helped you out.'

The atmosphere warmed up again. The lad had a way with language. '*Ha sciolto lo scilinguagnolo*' people commented around us. His popular directness had been the right thing.

'Ah bravo!' replied Cipolla. 'I like you, *giovanotto*. Would a smart lad like you believe me if I said I had my eyes on you from the beginning? People like you are my type, they're people I can work with. It's clear there's no messing with a man like you. You do as you want. Or have you ever not done what you wanted to? Or done what you didn't want to do? Just think, my friend, what a laugh it would be, how you could give yourself an easy time, not always having to show you can handle yourself, not always having to account for both your will and your actions. A division of labour would be useful, you know, the American system? *Sa'*? You know what I'm talking about? For example, are you inclined to stick your tongue out at this refined and respectable public we have around us, your whole tongue, that would be, right to the root of it?'

'No,' said the lad, not at all friendly. 'I don't want to do that. It would be proof of a poor upbringing.'

'It wouldn't prove anything,' responded Cipolla, 'for you would just be doing it. All respect to your upbringing, but in my view before I can count to three you'll do a U-turn and stick out your tongue at the assembled company, further than you ever thought you could.'

He looked at him, and as he did so his piercing eyes seemed to sink deeper into their sockets. '*Uno*,' he said, and took up the riding whip he'd loosened from his arm and cracked it once through the air. The lad turned to face the audience and stuck his tongue out so far, with such effort, and for so long, that one could see he could never have managed more by way of sticking out a tongue. Then, with no expression on his face, he resumed his previous position.

'It was me.' Cipolla made fun of him, with a twinkle in his eye and a nod of his head in the direction of the boy. '*Bè*... so, OK, it was me.' Then, leaving the audience to their own conclusion, he turned back to the small round table, poured himself a drink, evidently brandy, from the flask and knocked it back with a professional swagger.

The children roared with laughter. They understood almost nothing of the words that had been exchanged; but what had gone on between the peculiar man up there and someone from the audience was so comical that they were thoroughly amused, and since they had no definite idea in advance of what the evening would bring, they were ready to find this a terrific start. As for us, we just exchanged a look, and I remember that, I somehow couldn't help it, I found myself imitating the sound of Cipolla's riding whip cracking through the air. For the rest it was clear that people didn't know what they were supposed to make of such a bizarre opening to an evening of conjuring tricks, and hadn't properly understood what had inclined the *giovanotto*, who was in a way one of them, suddenly to turn his rudeness against them, the public. They found the young lad's behaviour ridiculous, didn't bother about him any more and switched their attention to the artist, who, as he walked back from his refreshment table, resumed his discourse in the following manner: 'Ladies and Gentlemen,' he said in his asthmatic-metallic voice, 'you just saw me somewhat niggled by the lesson this optimistic young linguist wanted to teach me. ('*Questo linguista de belle speranze*,' was how he put it, and people laughed at the dig at the boy's gabbiness.) You need to take into account that I'm a man with some self-esteem. I think highly of myself. I find it tasteless for someone to wish me good evening in any tone other than serious and polite, and there's really very little reason to do the opposite. When someone wishes me good evening, then in that case he's wishing himself a good one, for the public will only have a good evening if I do, and therefore it was a very good move on the part of this young lad, whom all the girls of Torre di Venere go for, to give me immediate proof that I'm having a good evening and can do without whatever he wishes me.' (He didn't stop needling the young man.) 'I'd go so far as to boast that I have almost nothing but good evenings. Occasionally one doesn't go so well, but that's rare. My profession is a difficult one and my health is not the most robust; I suffer from a slight physical defect that made it impossible for me to fight in the war for the greatness of my country. It's only with strength of mind and soul that I can master life, which is to say, achieve self-mastery, and I flatter myself to have aroused with my work the interest and respect of the educated public. The top newspapers were full of praise, *Corriere della Sera* went so far to do me justice as to call me a phenomenon, and in Rome I had the honour to see the Duce's brother among my audience when I gave a performance there one evening. Given the usual reactions that people in some socially grand, glamorous place have been inclined to grant me, I believed that in Torre di Venere—let's face it, a comparatively less important place' (people laughed as he took a dig at poor Torre) '—I scarcely believed I should have to put up with, and deal with personally, a lad spoilt by too much attention from the ladies. Torre di Venere should not deny me the same quality of reception as elsewhere.' Once again the young *donnaiolo*, the local cock of the roost, paid a price Cipolla didn't tire of exacting. The animosity and the rather brutal over-reaction with which he attacked the youngster starkly contrasted with the self-esteem and the worldly successes he vaunted. For sure, the lad served as an object of fun, of the kind that Cipolla liked to seek out every evening and put on the spot. There was that simple side to it. And yet in his intensity there was a real hatred. You could understand it in human terms if you compared the bodies of the two men. There was the explanation, the reason why the deformed man on the stage kept alluding to the good-looking boy's success with women. Obvious, wasn't it.

'Right then, let's get this show on road!' he added. 'To do that just let me make myself a bit more comfortable.'

And he walked over to the coat-stand to divest himself.

'*Parla benissimo,*' someone near us volunteered. Our entertainer hadn't done anything yet, but the way he spoke already counted for something. He knew how to impress. 'He's a superb speaker.' For people from southern countries talking is part of what makes life a joy, and they rate it much more highly as a social skill than people in the north. In these southern peoples their mother tongue binds them together as a nation, and there are grand models that are revered. So that something that offers a model at a certain cultural level, while being more entertaining and relaxed, commands the same respect and enjoyment as do correct grammatical forms and pronunciation. People relish talking and they relish listening—and not without passing judgement. For it's a measure of personal status, how a person speaks; those who are lazy and make mistakes are despised, elegance and competence invite other people's respect, which is why our little conjuror, insofar as he wants to have an effect on others, goes in for choice turns of phrase and forms them with care. In this respect at least, then, Cipolla had clearly made an impression, although he was not at all the kind of man whom the Italians, in a mixture of moral and aesthetic judgement, would call '*simpatico*'.

After he'd taken off his top hat, scarf and cloak, he was left wearing his frock coat. Tugging at his cuffs, which were fastened with large buttons, setting his humbug of a sash to rights, he came back to the front of the stage. He had really ugly hair, that is to say: the top of his skull was almost bald, and the hair, blackened with wax, was thinly combed over from the parting to cover his head; it looked as if it were stuck on; meanwhile the hair at his temples, also dyed black, was brushed forward in the direction of his eyes. It was the hairstyle of a rather old-fashioned circus director, absurd, but entirely fitted to the style of personality he was projecting; moreover he carried it off with such self-confidence that the public, whether or not inclined to find it comic, held back and remained silent. The 'slight physical defect' he'd been talking about a while ago was now all too clearly visible, even if still unclear as to its actual nature; his chest was too high, as is usual in such cases, but the cause of the trouble in his back seemed not to sit in the usual place, between the shoulders, but lower down, by way of a deformity that bent his posterior and his hips forwards, which didn't stop him walking but made him look grotesque and peculiarly repugnant with every step. But as it happened his mention of it drew the sting from his misery, as it were, and you could feel how the whole room became finely sensitive to his pain, as is the way with civilized people.

'At your service!' said Cipolla. 'If we may presume on your agreement we will begin our programme with a few mathematical exercises.'

Arithmetic? That didn't sound like magical tricks. There was already a suspicion that the man was sailing under a false flag; it only remained unclear which would have been the correct one. I began to feel sorry for the children; but they were happy for every second that they could stay in his presence.

The numbers game that Cipolla now set up was as simple as the point of it was obscure. He began by fixing a sheet of paper and a drawing pen to the top-right corner of the board. Lifting up the paper, he wrote something in chalk underneath. He kept talking the whole time, wanting to ensure with a constant barrage of commentary and encouragement that no aridity would mar the performance. In this his skill with words revealed him to be an excellent master of ceremonies. He was never stuck for a new topic to chat about. It was his way of working, to continue to erase the distance between the podium and the audience. The weird exchange with the young fisherman had been the first move; he went on to call members of the public up on to the stage, and as they approached the wooden stairs he personally came down to greet them and make contact; and it all delighted the children. I don't know how far the fact that he then instantly got into tension with different individuals was intended and part of his system, but he remained very serious and sullen each time it happened.

Anyway the audience, at least the popular contingent of it, seemed to be of the opinion that it was all part of the show.

So after he had written down whatever it was, and covered it with the sheet of paper, he expressed the wish that two people might come up on to the stage to help carry out the proposed mathematical task. He gave the audience to understand that they shouldn't fear any difficulties, and even those not so good at maths would perfectly fit the bill. As usual no one spoke up, and Cipolla held back from imposing on the distinguished section of the audience. He addressed the ordinary people and turned to two really loutish youths with standing places at the back of the auditorium, called on them to come up, gave them courage, said he thought it reprehensible that they should just stand idly gawping and not make any attempt to please the audience, and really got them going. They made their clumsy way to the front through the middle aisle, climbed the steps and, grinning awkwardly to the cheers of their pals, took up a position in front of the blackboard. Cipolla joked a while more with them, praised the heroic proportions of their limbs, the size of their hands, which were just made to perform the service asked of them before the assembled company, and then gave one of them the piece of chalk and told him simply to write down the numbers that would be called out to him. But the person said he didn't know how to write. '*Non so scrivere*,' he said in a coarse voice, and his companion added: 'Me neither.'

Heaven knows whether they were telling the truth or just wanted to make a fool of Cipolla. In any case, the latter was in no mood to join in the amusement that their confessions provoked. He was offended. They disgusted him. He was sitting at that moment with his legs crossed in one of the rush chairs in the middle of the stage and smoking another cigarette from the cheap packet, which tasted visibly so much better to him after the second brandy to which he'd just helped himself, while the two idiots were stomping their way up on to the stage. Once again he inhaled deeply and then let the smoke stream out between bared teeth. See-sawing his foot up and down, seized by complete revulsion, like a man who must remove himself from the presence of such a contemptible event and rescue his dignity, he looked past the two dishonourable dopes who were rejoicing and even looked past the audience; he was staring into the void.

'It's a scandal,' he said coldly and bitterly. 'Go back to your places! Everyone can write in Italy. Italy is a great power that has no room for ignorance and darkness. It's a bad joke to make an admission like that out loud, in front of an international audience, for you not only humiliate yourselves but also create a bad reputation for the government and the country. If Torre di Venere is really the last corner of the Fatherland in which even elementary schooling has failed, then I would have to regret my choice to come here, for I ought to have known how far behind Rome it stands in importance in this and that respect…'

Here he was interrupted by the lad with the Nubian haircut and the jacket over the shoulder, whose willingness to intervene, as people could see, had only temporarily receded and who now, carrying his head high, presented himself as the knight errant of his little town.

'That's enough,' he said. 'That's enough jokes about Torre. We all come from here and we won't put up with anyone making fun of our town in front of foreigners. Also these two are our friends. They may not be academics, but they are for all that much better fellows than perhaps some others in this room. I mean there are those who make a big deal of Rome but it's not as if they founded it.'

That was brilliant. The young man really had a way with words. The drama was all very entertaining, although it postponed the

start of the actual programme more and more. It's always grip-
ping to witness a verbal spat. It gives some people a kick, and they
experience a kind of schadenfreude by way of not being part of
the conversation themselves; others get worried and excited, and
I understand them very well, even though I had the impression at
that time that everything had been more or less agreed in advance,
and that both the illiterate dimwits and the *giovanotto* in the jacket
were in league with the artist, with the aim of making a scene.
The children listened absorbedly. They understood nothing, but
the tone took their breath away. To that extent it was a magical
evening, albeit an Italian one. They found it absolutely topping,
and kept saying so.

Cipolla got up, and with two thrusts of his hips moved swiftly
to the front of the stage.

'Won't you just look at that!' he said with a kind of grim sincerity. 'Look who's back! The youngster who always has the right
words on the tip of his tongue!' (He used an Italian expression,
sulla linguaccia, which meant his tongue was furred up, which made
everyone laugh.) 'Off you go, you two,' he said to the two dolts.
'I don't need you any more, I have enough to do with this good
fellow, with this *torregiano di Venere*, with this gatekeeper of Venus,
who no doubt envisages tender gestures of feminine gratitude in
return for his protectiveness towards the town…'

'Ah, *non scherzamo*! Let's talk about it seriously, no more joking,'
cried the lad. His eyes were blazing, and truly he made a gesture
as if he wanted to throw off his jacket and move on to a more
direct kind of encounter.

That was no great tragedy for Cipolla. Unlike us, who exchanged
worried glances, he was dealing with a fellow Italian on home
ground. He stayed cool, showed his perfect superiority. Looking
towards the audience, he smiled and gestured with his head

towards the fighting cockerel, called upon the onlookers to be the witnesses of a belligerence by which the pugilist only revealed the primitiveness of his life-form. And then another extraordinary thing happened that put that superiority in a sinister light and in some shameful and inexplicable way turned the aggression the scene gave off into something absurd.

Cipolla came closer still to the lad, and in a peculiar way stared into his eyes. There were the wooden steps that, to the left of us, led down from the stage into the auditorium and he came halfway down, so that he was standing right in front of the querulous youngster, but a bit above him. The riding whip hung from his arm.

'You're not in the mood for jokes, my son,' he said. 'That's understandable, for any one can see that something's not right with you. Your tongue alone showed symptoms of acute gastric disorder. As for your mouth, wash it out, I would. When someone feels the way you do they shouldn't go out in the evening to a show, and you yourself, I know, were in two minds whether or not to stay in bed and wrap up warm. It was silly to drink so much of that white wine this afternoon. It was terribly sour. Now you've got such cramps in your stomach that you're doubling up with pain. Go ahead, do what you have to! There's a certain relief that comes from the body giving way to a convulsion in the gut.'

As he was, from one word to the next, calmly driving home this message, involving himself unremittingly in the young man's business, his eyes, fastened on the other man's eyes, seemed to stand out of their sockets. They were somehow burning and feeble at the same time, those weird eyes, and it was clear that it was not only out of manly pride that his partner didn't retract his glance. Nor all of a sudden was there a sign of his earlier cockiness to be seen in his suntanned face. He fastened on the maestro open-mouthed, and that wide-open mouth as it smiled looked woeful, as if he had lost control.

'Bend over and clutch your stomach!' repeated Cipolla. 'What else can you do? An upset stomach makes a person clutch his stomach. Just because you're being told to do so, there's no need to resist what comes naturally.'

The young man slowly lifted his arms, and as he crossed them over and pressed them against his belly his body bent over, downwards and from side to side, ever deeper; his knees turned inwards against each other and his feet were all over the place so that in the end, a picture of screwed-up agony, he was almost crawling on the floor. Cipolla left him like that for a few seconds before briefly cracking the riding whip through the air and returned his protruding figure to the little round table, where he knocked back a brandy.

'*Il boit beaucoup*,' insisted a woman behind us. Was that all she noticed, that he drank a lot? We weren't sure how far the public realized what was going on. The lad was standing up straight again, with rather an embarrassed smile, as if he didn't really know what had happened to him. The audience had followed the tense scene and applauded when it was over, with people even calling out, 'Bravo, Cipolla!' and, to the young man, 'Bravo, *giovanotto*!' Apparently they didn't take the resolution of the quarrel as a defeat for the youngster, they cheered him on as an actor who had made a good job of an awkward role. That was true. His way of doubling up in pain had been extremely impressive, as if with so much vividness he had been playing to the gallery. It was really a *coup de théâtre*. But I'm not sure how far the behaviour of the audience was attributable to human fellow-feeling, in which people from the southern countries are superior to us, and how far it rested on actual insight into what was at stake.

The maestro, refreshed, had lit another cigarette. It was time to resume the experiment with the numbers. There was no difficulty in finding a young man sitting in one of the back rows who was prepared to write down the dictated figures on the blackboard. We even knew him; the whole evening had something of a family gathering about it, since we recognized so many faces. He was an assistant in the greengrocer's and general store on the main road and had several times given us good service. He handled the chalk with all the facility you'd expect from someone working in a commercial business, even while Cipolla, who had stepped down to our level, was moving with his awkward posture through the audience and memorizing two-, three- and four-digit sums offered by the people he asked freely to think of a number, whereupon he called them out for his part to the young shopkeeper, who wrote them down one beneath the other. At the same time, as they went back and forth, it was all a bit of lark, with a lot of ad-libbing, designed to entertain the public. It had to happen that to ask his question the artist fastened on some visitor from elsewhere, who couldn't manage the numbers in Italian, and whom he went out of his way to treat chivalrously, to the polite amusement of the locals, whom he then embarrassed by asking them to act as the interpreters for sums given in English and French. Some volunteered numbers that depicted great years in Italian history. Cipolla grasped them straightaway, and whenever he mentioned them again added some patriotic sentiment. Someone said: 'Naught!' and the maestro, deeply offended, as always, by any attempt to take him for a fool, responded over his shoulder that that was a figure of less than two digits, whereupon another joker yelled: 'Naught, naught!' and enjoyed sure-fire success with the merry crowd with his allusion to a lower part of the body. You can guarantee an effect like that in the south. But the maestro himself, dignified, held back, even though he'd pretty much invited the lewdness himself; with a shrug of his shoulders he just gave this sum too to the scribe to include.

When there were about fifteen numbers of various lengths on the board, Cipolla asked for them to be added together. Anyone who was good at maths could work it out in their heads without writing anything down, but people were free to use pencil and paper. While they worked on it, Cipolla sat on his chair alongside the board, pulled a few faces and smoked, with the complacent, fastidious, affected behaviour of a crippled man. It wasn't long before the five-figure answer was ready. Someone communicated it, another corroborated it, a third person came up with something close, a fourth agreed with the first two. Cipolla stood up, brushed some ash off his frock coat, lifted up the sheet of paper in the right-hand corner of the board and let everyone see what he had written down. The right figure, totalling almost one million, could be seen there. He'd guessed it in advance.

Astonishment and much clapping. The children were overwhelmed. How did he do that, they wanted to know. We had them understand that it was a trick, not immediatcly to be understood, after all the man was a conjuror. Now they knew what was meant by a *soirée* with a practitioner of the art of magic. How the fisherman came to double up in pain and how the final result was already on the blackboard—that was fantastic, and we noticed with some concern that, despite their feverish eyes and the fact that it was already almost half past ten, it would be very hard to take them away. There would be tears. And yet it was clear that this hunchback was not performing magic, at least not in the sense of performing a skill, and that none of this was for children. Again, I don't know what exactly the audience thought; only that when it came to came to asking individuals freely to choose a number, evidently it was very doubtful it had happened that way; some of the people he asked may well have answered for themselves, but on the whole it was clear Cipolla had picked his own recruits, and that the process, focused on reaching the number he'd already written down, was under his control—in the midst of which one still had to admire his quick mathematical brain, if admiration was hardly appropriate for whatever other strange things were going on. Add into the bargain the elements of patriotism and easily injured dignity; it was all very well if the locals were in their element and felt it was harmless and were happy for the jokes to continue; for people coming from outside the mixture of the two was oppressive.

In fact, Cipolla himself took care that anyone with half a thought in his head would have no doubt as to the character of his performance, while not mentioning any names or defining his art. He certainly addressed it, for he talked incessantly, but only in a vague, pretentious way that sounded like self-promotion. For a while he continued along the experimental path he had started out on, made the calculations more complicated by way of including subtractions, multiplications and divisions in the total, and then simplified it in the extreme, to show us how it worked. He had people 'advise' him of a number, and that was the one he'd written down before under the sheet of paper. It almost always succeeded. Someone admitted that he'd actually had a different number in mind but that in that moment the maestro's riding whip had come cracking through the air and the number that then issued from him was the one found on the board. Cipolla's shoulders rocked with laughter. He faked astonishment at the ingenuity of his partners in the audience, but these compliments had something denigrating and mocking about them, I don't think they would have given any pleasure to the people concerned, although they smiled and took the applause to be partly directed at them. Nor did I have the impression that the artist was much liked by his audience. I got the sense of a certain revulsion; they were unwilling to go along with him; but it barely needs saying that politeness holds such impulses within bounds. Cipolla's know-how, his rigorous self-belief, could hardly fail to make an impression, and even the riding whip, in my view, further contributed to keep the revolt below ground.

From experiments with numbers he moved on to cards. He took two packs out of his pocket, and what I retain of the moment is that the fundamental and exemplary trick he worked up out of them was this: from one pack he drew three cards, blind, which he then hid in an inside pocket of his frock coat, and then the guinea pig from the audience drew exactly these three cards from the second pack held out to him—they weren't always exactly the right ones—it happened that only two were correct, but in the majority of instances Cipolla triumphed when he produced his three cards for the audience, and modestly accepted the applause which, for better, or for worse, saluted the powers he had. A young man in the front row, to the right of us, an Italian with a proudly chiselled face, put up his hand and insisted he was determined to make choices that would clearly be his own, and that he would consciously resist any and every attempt to influence him. What might be the outcome of that, he asked Cipolla. Answered the maestro: 'You will make my task a bit more difficult. Your resistance won't change anything about the result. Freedom exists and so does the will exist; but freedom of the will doesn't exist, for a will that aims at its own freedom is acting in a void. You are free to take a card or not. But if you do take a card then you will take the right one—and this is all the more certain the more you try to retain personal control over the matter.'

One had to admit that, had he wanted to muddy the waters and create confusion in the man's very soul, he couldn't have chosen his words better. His opponent hesitated nervously before he made his choice. He drew one card and immediately demanded to know whether it was among the hidden ones. 'What are you up to?' cried Cipolla, amazed. 'Why only do half the job?' But then, since the stubborn fellow insisted on this initial test: '*È servito*. Here it is, with my compliments.' The entertainer made an unusually servile gesture and produced his three cards, holding them fan-wise, without looking at them himself. The one on the left was the one the man had drawn.

The freedom fighter sat down angrily, to the applause of the auditorium. To what extent Cipolla supplemented his innate gifts with little mechanical tricks and sleights of hand only the devil knew. Given some kind of prestidigitation, the expansive curiosity of everyone present bound them together in the enjoyment of a phenomenal piece of entertainment. They had to recognize a professional competence no one could deny. '*Lavora bene!*' We could hear people all around us saying he was doing a good job, and it meant that being right plain and simple triumphed over antipathy and silent outrage.

Now, after his last, fragmentary, but for that reason all the more impressive success, Cipolla had once again fortified himself with a brandy. 'He drinks a lot,' that was perfectly true, and it wasn't good to see. But evidently he needed liquor and cigarettes to keep up and refresh his concentration, which, as he had himself suggested, was faced with intense demands in multiple different contexts. He really looked terrible in between, hollow-eyed and sunken-cheeked. Each time his tipple set him to rights, and his talk followed. Meanwhile the smoke he inhaled billowed grey from his lungs. It was like a stream of life and an overbearing challenge to anyone who watched him. I know for certain that at some point he switched from card tricks to mind games; to playing the kind of games with mass perception that rest on the supra- or sub-rational capacities in human nature, on intuition and 'magnetic' transfer; briefly, he offered the audience revelations, of a low kind. But I no longer know how one trick followed another precisely. Nor will I bore you with a description of these experiments. Everyone knows them, everyone has taken part. They consist in pouncing on hidden objects, or blindly carrying out a series of actions, whereby something is transferred from one organism to another. The result leads down paths not known to science. Watching experiments like that, everyone has responded with a mixture of curiosity and contempt; everyone has had, even while shaking their heads, their little insights into the ambivalent, impure and inextricable character of the occult, which, so far as those human beings who have a gift are concerned, always vexingly inclines them to get mixed up with humbug and a bit of cheating on the side, without this element proving anything against the genuine nature of other constituent parts of the whole dubious amalgam. I would only say that so much more is at stake, that the impressions run deeper in every direction, when a Cipolla is the chief executive of this dark art and its principal actor. He was sitting, his back to the public, at the rear of the stage, smoking, while somewhere in the auditorium, unseen, the deals were reached that he had ordered, the object was passed from hand to hand which he would then take out of its hiding place and do with whatever he had planned in advance. It was typical of how he groped his way forwards, now driven onwards to reach his goal, now stumbling, stopping to listen, tapping out his path like a blind man and then with an abrupt change of direction correcting himself. This was the display he put on when he was being guided by the hand by a leader in the know, who had been advised to maintain himself in a posture of complete bodily submission but to keep his thoughts on what had been agreed. He had his head thrown back and his hands stretched out in front of him as he made his way in a zigzag through the auditorium. The roles seemed to have been swapped, the flow of the current reversed, and the artist indicated the change with an ever more fluent stream of talk. The passive, receptive one, the one whose will was switched off and who had to carry out tasks at the command of another person, hovered somewhere in the air of the silent room; he had for so long been giving out the orders and having people do *his* will, but now he became the passive partner; although he insisted that in the end it didn't make any difference. The ability to divest oneself of one's personality, to empty oneself of any inner life, to become a tool, to obey, in the fullest and most unconditional sense of the word, was, he insisted, only the reverse side of that other impulse to exercise one's will and have people obey; it was one and the same capacity, to give orders and to obey, together they comprised a single principle, an indivisible unity; the person capable of giving orders knows just as well how to obey; the one idea is included in the other, just as Leader and People are included one in the other, but the real achievement, the incredibly rigorous and exhausting achievement, was indeed his own, as Leader and Instigator, since in him will became obedience and obedience will, his own person was the birthplace of both, he said, and that was why his calling was so hard. He stressed unremittingly and often that it was extraordinarily hard for him, probably to explain his desperate need for refreshment and his frequent reaching for the glass.

He tapped his way about like a blind seer, guided and led by the secret will of the public. He drew a pin set with gemstones out of the shoes of an Englishwoman, where it had been hidden, bore it stumblingly and unfailingly towards another woman—it was Signora Angiolieri—and, falling to his knees, handed it over to her with prearranged words which, though he had them vividly in mind, were still not so easy to find; for it had been agreed they would be in French. 'I give you a present as a sign of my esteem for you,' is what he had to say, and it struck us that there might be some mischief in the difficulty of the assignment; a dichotomy became apparent in what we wished for, between the hope to see this miracle man succeed and the longing to see a man with such pretensions humiliated. But it was most remarkable how Cipolla, on his knees before Madame Angiolieri, trying out various per-mutations, was struggling to find the one he had been given. 'I have something to say,' he said, 'and I can feel very clearly what it's about. At the same time I feel that, were I to let it pass my lips, it would be false. At all costs beware of helping me by giving me any kind of involuntary sign,' he cried, when surely what he actually hoped for was the opposite... '*Pensez très fort!*' he cried all of a sudden in bad French and then came out with the required sentence, albeit in Italian, but in such a way that the most impor-tant word and the final word came out in that related language which he probably didn't know well at all, and instead of '*vener-azione*' he said '*vénération*', sticking a nasal 'n' on the end which was quite impossible—a partial success, which, coming after the achievements of having found the pin, having made his way to the woman destined to receive it, and kneeling before her, made an almost more vivid impression than had he achieved complete victory, and people clapped in amazement.

Cipolla stood up and wiped the sweat from his brow. You understand that I was only giving one example of his work when I told the story of the pin—it is one that has stayed particularly in my memory. But he often varied the basic line and wove it through his experiments, and much time was taken up with related improvi-sations, in which he was helped a great deal by physical contact with the public. In particular he seemed to draw inspiration from the person of our landlady; she enticed out of him some dazzling pronouncements: 'It hasn't escaped me, signora,' he told her, 'that there's some connection in you to something special and distinguished. Anyone who has the eyes to see it can make out around your charming brow a halo, which, if I am not mistaken, was once stronger than it is today, a slowly fading halo... No, don't say a word! Don't help me! Beside you sits your husband, isn't that so,' and he turned to the silent Mr Angiolieri. 'You are the husband of this woman, and your happiness is complete. But memories force their way into this happiness... princely memories.... The past, signora, plays a significant part in your present life, as it seems to me. You knew a king... was it not in past days that a king crossed your path?'

'Well no,' said the provider of our midday meal, and her golden-brown eyes sparkled in the noble pallor of her face.

'No? No, not a king. I was speaking as it were while the thought was still crude and unrefined. Not a king, not a prince—but a prince even so, a king of higher realms. It was a great artist at whose side you once... You want to contradict me, but you can't do it with total conviction, you can only do it half-ways. So, I know! It was a great, world-famous woman artist, whose friendship you enjoyed in your tender youth and whose sacred memory overshadows and transfigures your whole life... her name? Is it necessary to pronounce the name of a woman whose renown has long since merged with that of the Fatherland and, together with the Fatherland, is immortal. Eleonora Duse,' he concluded in a ceremonious half-whisper.

The little woman, overcome, shrank into herself. She nodded. The applause made it seem as if she were being given a national medal. Almost everyone in the auditorium, the present guests of the Casa Eleonora chief among them, knew of Mrs Angiolieri's significant past and could therefore substantiate the maestro's intuition. It was only a question of how much he himself had known, from when he first arrived in Torre and put his professional ear to the ground, how much he was able to take from that... But I have absolutely no reason to suspect on rational grounds the abilities that before our eyes would become his undoing...

Now, though, there was an interval, and the man who had us in his power withdrew. I must admit that almost since I began telling this tale I've been afraid of reaching this point in my report. It's mostly not very difficult to read people's thoughts, and here it is very easy. Without fail you will ask me why we didn't at some point leave—and I owe you an answer. I don't understand it and I really don't know what to reply. At the time it must definitely have been after eleven, and probably even later. The children were asleep. The last series of experiments had been really boring for them, so nature found it easy to insist on its rights. They slept on our laps, our little girl on mine, the boy on his mother's knee. In a way that was comforting, but also once again a reason to take pity on them and a warning to get them home to bed. I can assure you that we wanted to heed it, we really wanted to obey this warning, our hearts were touched. We woke up the poor little things to tell them we had decided it was high time to return home. But their bitter protest began from the moment they came to, and you know how impossible it is to overcome the outrage children feel at being dragged away from a pleasant event. We would have had to drag them. It was so much fun to be watching the conjuror, they protested, we couldn't know what might come next, the very least one could do was wait and see how he began the second half, they would happily have a bit of a nap in between, only please not to go home, please not to have to go to bed, so long as this topping evening was still continuing.

We gave in, even if, as it seemed to us, we were only doing it for the moment, just for a while, for the time being. That we stayed was unforgivable, but almost equally inexplicable. Did we believe we had to say B, after we had said A and brought the children here, which had been altogether a mistake? I don't find that satisfactory. Was it that we ourselves were enjoying the show? Yes and no, our feelings for maestro Cipolla were of a very mixed kind, but those, if I'm not wrong, were the feelings of the whole audience, and still no one left. Were we the victims of a spell that emanated from this man, with his odd way of earning his living, and which weakened our resolution? His powers reached us also when he was not following the programme; the power was there also between tricks. But it might just as well be that we must reckon with our pure curiosity. Who wouldn't want to know how an evening that had begun like that would continue, and anyway Cipolla had left the stage making announcements that left us to conclude that he had by no means exhausted his repertoire and we might expect something on a higher level again, given the impact it would make upon us.

But all of that is not enough, or it's not everything. The right thing to do, above all, would have been to answer the question why we didn't leave now with another asking why we hadn't departed from Torre itself long since. In my view it is one and the same question, and to wriggle out of it I might try maintaining that I have already answered it. Our memorable evening was just as tense and peculiar, just as unsettling, offensive and off-putting as things were in Torre generally, indeed even more so: this auditorium concentrated in itself all the weirdness, all the tenseness, all the outrageousness which seemed to charge the atmosphere of our stay; this man, whose return to the stage we were awaiting, seemed to us the personification of it all; and since we hadn't left for good it would have been illogical, so to speak, to leave on this particular occasion. You may accept that as the explanation of our lethargy, or not! I have nothing better to offer.

The ten-minute interval became something closer to twenty. The children, who had stayed awake and who were delighted with our indulgence, knew how to fill every one of those minutes to their satisfaction. They refreshed their acquaintance with the local people, with Antonio, Guiscardo and the paddle boat man. They cupped their hands and cried in the direction of the fishermen sentiments they had roughly heard from us: 'Hope you catch a lot of super fish tomorrow!' 'Make sure those nets are full!' They called out to Mario, the under-waiter from the Esquisito: '*Mario, una cioccolata e biscotti!*' '*Subito!* A hot chocolate and some biscotti coming up!' He took notice this time and replied with a smile. We acquired reasons to keep this friendly and rather wistful, melancholy smile in our memory.

The interval came to an end, the gong sounded, the public, immersed in chatting, filled the room, the children sat upright in their chairs, hands in their laps, straining for what was about to happen. The stage had remained open to view. Cipolla strode up to the front and straight away began to introduce the second half of his show as if he were giving a lecture.

Let me put it in a nutshell: this misshapen, self-confident fellow was the most powerful hypnotist that I've ever come across in my life. If he had, with regard to the nature of his art, thrown sand in the eyes of the authorities and announced himself as a conjuror, evidently the point was to evade police regulations, which fundamentally outlawed the commercial practice of his talents. Perhaps it's the norm in Italy to draw a veil over such cases, and the form is they are officially tolerated or half-tolerated. In any case, our entertainer had from the beginning hardly tried to disguise the real nature of his practice, and the second half of his programme was now entirely openly and exclusively focused on a special experiment, a demonstration of loss of will and its recovery, even if the patter was still dominated by euphemisms. In a wearisome series of comic, exciting, amazing experiments which were still in full flow at midnight, the audience had sight, from the unprepossessing to the uncanny, of everything by way of phenomena that this natural-supernatural sphere had to offer, and as grotesque details came to light the public followed with laughter and applause, slapping their knees and shaking their heads. They were clearly under the spell of a personality resolute with self-belief, despite the fact that, at least as it seemed to me, they were not without a feeling of revulsion at the disrespect, the humiliation of individuals and of the whole audience on which all of Cipolla's triumphs rested.

Two things played the leading role in these triumphs: the little glass of brandy he knocked back and the riding whip with the claw handle. The former had always to serve to bring out his daemonic streak, for otherwise, as it seemed, exhaustion threatened, and that might have created a feeling of human concern for the man, had he not had in his hand that whip that was an obscene symbol of his mastery over others. It was broadsword with which, as he swished it through the air, he subordinated us all to his overbearing intentions, and its effect forbade any milder response than, bewildered and with one's own will overruled, to succumb. Did he want for something more tender in our response? Was he also still hoping to arouse our sympathy? Did he want everything? Something he said stuck in my mind, which made me think he did feel such resentment towards others. He showed it when, at the climax of his experiments, he had, with motions of his hand and the exercise of his aura, reduced a young man, who had put himself at his disposal and who had already shown himself to be particularly receptive to such influences, to a state of utter catalepsy, to the extent that he could not only lay this man whom he had plunged into a deep sleep across two chairs, one under the neck, the other under the feet, but he could also sit on the body without that seeming corpse, stiff as a board, giving way. The sight of that fiend in a frock coat, squatting on the figure of a man he had turned to wood, was unbelievable and appalling, and the audience, having formed the impression that the victim of this scientific divertissement must be suffering, sighed in pity: '*poveretto!*' Well-wishers called out: 'The poor man!' '*Poveretto!*' repeated a bitter Cipolla, mockingly. 'You're directing your sympathies at the wrong man, ladies and gentlemen. *Sono io, il poveretto*. I'm the poor man here. I'm the one who has to put up with everything.' People took notice of what he'd said. Fine, perhaps he was the one who bore the costs of the entertainment and conceivably may also have taken upon himself the bodily pains which showed in the young man as pitiful facial contortions. But appearances did not suggest that, and people are not inclined to level the word *poveretto* at someone who is suffering so that others can be debased.

I've run ahead in my story and abandoned the actual sequence of events. Still today my head is full of memories of Maestro The-things-I-have-to-put-up-with. It's just that I don't know how to order those memories and it's not about them. What I do know is that the big, elaborate stunts, the ones that invited the most applause, made less of an impression on me than the small ones that were soon over. The phenomenon of the young man used as a bench to sit on only came to mind just now because of the reproach attached to it… That an older woman, asleep on one of the rush chairs, should have been coaxed by Cipolla into believing she was visiting India, and reported back out of her trance in a very lively fashion of her adventures on land and water, worried me far less, I was much more stunned when, immediately after the break, a tall, broadly built gentleman of military appearance could no longer lift his arm, only because the hunchback, cracking his riding whip through the air, told him he wouldn't be able to do it any more. I can still see the face of this solid, imposing moustachioed *colonello* before me, the way he was smiling and gritting his teeth as he struggled to regain his forfeited freedom of movement. The business was all very confusing! He seemed to want to but he couldn't; but what he couldn't do, apparently, was stop wanting, and what was at stake was the immobilizing entanglement of the will within itself, blocking freedom, as our spellbinder had already mockingly predicted would happen to the gentleman from Rome.

I'm even less disposed to forget the scene with Mrs Angiolieri, the way the comedy was so moving and seemed to happen on another plane. The maestro had no doubt spotted her ethereal vulnerability to his power when he took a first brazen look around the room. He drew her literally out of her chair by casting a spell on her, drew her to him out of the row where she was sitting, and as he did so he gave Mr Angiolieri the task of calling out his wife's first name, as if to throw the weight of his very existence and his marital rights into the balance. With his husband's voice his task was to awaken in the soul of his life companion whatever might protect her virtue against black magic; and all this, on the part of Cipolla, was done to make his own light shine more brightly. Now it was all in vain! Cipolla, a little way off from the couple, gave a crack of his whip and the effect was that Mrs Angiolieri shook violently and turned her face to him. 'Sofronia!' cried Mr Angiolieri (and this was the first time he spoke it, and before that we had had no idea that Mrs Angiolieri's first name was Sofronia), and quite rightly he began to call her, because anyone could see she was in danger; his wife's face remained blank, turned towards the accursed maestro. The latter then, with the riding whip looped over his arm, began to work on his victim with all his ten long, yellow fingers, beckoning and signalling as if to draw her along as he stepped backwards. Whereupon Mrs Angiolieri, radiantly pale, got up from her seat, turned in the direction of her possessor and began to follow him as if disembodied. She looked like a ghost! Her face was moonstruck, her hands stiff, her fine hands lifted a little at the wrist, and as if she had her feet tied together she seemed slowly to glide out of her seat in the wake of her seducer… 'Call your wife, dear sir, do please call her!' insisted that horrific man. And Mr Angiolieri called out in a weak voice: 'Sofronia!' Oh yes, he went on calling her. He even put one hollow hand to his lips and waved with the other as he called, for his wife was moving further and further away from him. But the sad voice of love and duty echoed powerlessly in the wake of the lost woman, and in her moonstruck trance, deaf and out of her mind, Mrs Angiolieri was gliding towards that man, down the middle aisle, towards that hunchback with such animated fingers, in the direction of the exit. The impression was so complete and compelling that, had he wanted it, she would have followed her master to the end of the earth.

'*Accidente!*' cried Mr Angiolieri in real horror, and leapt up as the auditorium door was reached. 'Help! My wife is in danger!' However in the same moment, as it were, the maestro removed his victor's laurels and broke off. 'Enough, signora, my thanks to you,' he said, and with a comic gesture of chivalrousness offered his arm to the returnee from the clouds in order to deliver her back to Mr Angiolieri. 'My dear sir,' he greeted the latter, 'here is your lawful wedded wife! Unharmed, and together with my compliments, I return her to you for safekeeping. Protect with all

the strength you have as a man this treasure who is so thoroughly
your own, and may the realization that forces exist stronger than
reason, stronger than virtue, fan the flames of your vigilance!
Ordinarily such forces are exceptionally unlikely to go hand in
hand with high-mindedness and renunciation.'

Poor Mr Angiolieri, bald and silent! He didn't look as if he
could have managed to protect his heart's desire against even minor
daemonic forces, as compared with those here that were still creating havoc. Puffed up and assuming an air of gravity, the maestro
returned to the stage to applause that his eloquence had doubled
in volume. Not to put too fine a point on it, with this victory, if I
am not wrong, his authority had risen to such a point that he could
have made his audience dance—made them dance, indeed. I mean
that entirely literally, and it brought with it a certain letting-go, a
kind of late-night-neither-here-nor-there in people's minds, a col-
lapse of the critical faculties, as if people were drunk, which up to
that point had resisted the influence of the disagreeable man. It's
true he'd had to fight hard to gain complete control, particularly
against the recalcitrance of the young gentleman from Rome,
whose moral paralysis threatened to leave a dangerous example
in the public mind. But as the maestro was well aware of how
important hat example was, and clever enough to choose the place
of least resistance as his starting-point, he singled out that puny,
easily befuddled young fellow—the lad he'd shortly before turned
into a plank of wood—and had him begin the dancing. As soon
as the maestro even looked at him, this boy had a way of hurling
his upper body backwards as if he'd been struck by lightning and,
with his hands on the seams of his trousers, of falling into a state
of military somnambulism, creating the vision of one who was
willing to join in with any and every nonsense that would be asked
of him. He also seemed quite happy to conform and to be rid of

his pathetically meagre sense of himself; for he kept offering to take part in the experiments and evidently found it an honour to serve as a prime example of how to give up one's soul and lose one's will at a stroke. Even now he got up on the stage and it only took one crack of the whip for him to start tap-dancing at the maestro's bidding, which was to say flinging his emaciated limbs out in every direction in a kind of complacent ecstasy, with closed eyes and his head swaying.

Apparently people enjoyed watching and it didn't take long for others to join in. One well-dressed and another simply dressed lad began tap-dancing either side of him. At this point the gentleman from Rome spoke up and delivered a defiant challenge: whether the maestro would commit to teaching him to dance, even if he didn't want to.

'Even if you don't want to!' answered Cipolla in a tone that I will never forget. This frightful '*anche se non vuole!*' still rings in my ears. And so the struggle began. Cipolla, after downing a brandy and lighting a fresh cigarette, positioned the man from Rome somewhere in the middle aisle with his face turned towards the exit. He himself took up a position a short distance behind him and cracked his whip as he cried: '*Balla!*' His opponent didn't move. '*Balla!*' the maestro repeated determinedly, and clicked his fingers. 'Dance!' We could see how the young man's neck moved against his collar and how at the same time one of his hands lifted at the wrist and one of his heels turned outwards. But for a long time that's all there was, these signs of a jerky attempt to dance that now picked up momentum and now fell still. No one doubted that here the subject had taken a decision in advance to resist as hard as he could and that in his case an heroic stubbornness had to be overcome; this good man wanted to save the honour of the human race, he quivered, but he didn't dance, and the experiment ran to such a length that the maestro was obliged to divide his attention; every now and again he turned towards the stage and to the figures jiggling about up there and cracked his whip at them to keep them under control, even as, turning aside to the audience, he informed them that those energetic fellows wouldn't have any sense of tiredness afterwards, however long they kept dancing, for it wasn't actually they who were dancing but he himself. Then he returned to staring at the neck of the Roman gentleman, trying to outdo that firmness of will that was resisting his power.

We could see this firmness wavering with his repeated slashes of the whip and his incessant commands, could see it in a detached way, which was not free from emotional elements, not free from regret and cruel satisfaction. If I understood what was happening aright, it was the negativity of his position that made this man liable to be defeated. Probably one's soul can't live in a state of not wanting; not to want to do something is, in the end, not to lead a life; not to want something and never again to will anything at all, and thus to do what is required, these ideas are too closely related for the idea of freedom not to force its way into the melee, and this was the direction in which the maestro steered his interventions, between cracking his whip and barking orders, as he went for a mixture of effects, some that were secret to him and some that were bafflingly psychological. '*Balla!*' he said. 'Why torment yourself? Do you call this freedom—this self-rape? *Una ballatina!* Come on now, a little dance! Every part of you is longing to do it. Think how good it will be, finally to let your limbs do what they want! That's it, you're starting to dance! It's no struggle any more, you're enjoying it!' And that's how it was, the twitching and jiggling in the body of the man who was trying so hard to resist gained the upper hand, he lifted his arm, his knee, suddenly all his joints loosened up, he was throwing his limbs about, he was dancing, and so, while the people clapped, the maestro steered him towards the stage to line him up with the other jumping jacks. We could see his face now, the face of a man in defeat, up there on public display. He wore a broad smile and, with his eyes half-closed, was 'having fun'. It was a kind of consolation to see that things were easier for him now than in the time of his pride...

It may be said that his 'fall from grace' was the high point. With him the ice was broken, Cipolla's triumph unassailable; Circe's magic wand, the crack of that leather crop with its knob in the shape of a claw, its rule was without bounds. At that point which I have in mind, and which may have been some time after midnight, there were eight or ten people dancing on the little stage, but also in the auditorium there was all sorts going on, and an Anglo-Saxon woman with long teeth and a pince-nez had, without the master having bothered with her, emerged from the row where she was sitting in order to dance a tarantella in the middle aisle. All the while Cipolla sat slumped on a rush chair to the left of the podium, swallowed the smoke from his cigarette and arrogantly let it stream back out between his ugly teeth. Waving his foot and occasionally laughing so that his shoulders shook, he cast a glance at the relaxed, easy-going company and every now and again, half from behind, cracked his whip in the direction of one of those articulated toys who might be slacking. The children were awake at this time. I feel ashamed as I mention them. This was not a good place to be, for them least of all, and that we still hadn't taken them away I can only explain in terms of a certain infectiousness about the general atmosphere of letting go, which affected us too at that time of night. Nothing mattered any more. As a matter of fact, and thank goodness for that, they had no sense of how obscene this evening event had become. Their innocence never tired of delighting in the fact that they were allowed to stay up and watch a display like this, to be part of a conjuror's magic show. Several times they had fallen asleep on our laps for a quarter of an hour or so, and with red cheeks and rapt eyes were now laughing themselves silly over the jumps in the air which the man of the evening was making people do. They'd never imagined it could be so funny, and their clumsy little hands joined happily in every burst of applause. Yet nothing outdid the pleasure—they had their own way of leaping out of their seats—when Cipolla waved to their friend Mario, Mario from the Esquisito, using a familiar gesture from the lexicon of hand signals, moving his hand in front of his nose and alternately extending his index finger and crooking it.

Mario obeyed. I can still see him climbing the steps up to the maestro, who all the while kept beckoning him with his index finger, reducing the well-known gesture to comic absurdity. There was only one moment when the young man hesitated, and that I remember very well. During the evening he'd leant against a wooden pillar in the side aisle, either with his arms folded or with his hands in the pockets of his jacket, that was to the left of us, where the *giovanotto* with the military hairstyle was also standing and taking in the performance, so far as we could see, but without much amusement and heaven knows with how much understanding. On top of all that, it was evidently not a pleasure to be called to join in at the last moment. Nevertheless it was only too easy to grasp why he should respond when a man waved. That was part of his job; besides, it was surely a spiritual impossibility for a simple lad like that to have refused a summons from a Cipolla who, at that moment, was revelling in his success. Happily or not, he detached himself from his pillar, thanked those standing around and in front of him for making way, and ascended to the stage, a doubtful smile on his parted lips.

Imagine him to yourself as a stockily built young man aged twenty, with short, cropped hair, a low brow and heavily lidded eyes, the colour of which was an indistinct grey mixed with green and yellow elements. I know this exactly, for we had often spoken to him. The upper half of his face, his nose flat and peppered with freckles across the bridge, receded against the lower half, which was dominated by fat lips. When he spoke his moist teeth were visible, and these luxuriant lips, together with his hooded eyes, gave his countenance a look of primitive melancholy, which was exactly why we always had some sympathy for Mario. There was no question of his having a brutal look about him; you had only to look at the unusual slenderness and fineness of his hands, which struck even southerners as aristocratic, and which made it a pleasure to be served by him.

We knew him as a person without knowing him personally, if you will allow me the distinction. We saw him almost every day and were in tune with the rather dreamy, easily distracted way in which he could lose himself and which he hastily corrected with an excess of good service. He took the job seriously, and it was only the children who could make him smile. He wasn't morose, but he didn't flatter people, he wasn't specially trying to make himself liked, in fact he didn't care about it at all, evidently having no hope of finding favour. In any case he was someone who stayed in our minds, one of the insignificant details from a holiday that are often more memorable than many a grander moment. But we knew nothing more of his circumstances other than that his father was a humble clerk at the town hall and his mother took in washing.

The white jacket he wore to wait at table fitted him better than the worn-out suit, made of some thin, striped material, in which he now mounted the stage, not wearing a collar and tie round his neck but a flame-red silk cravat whose ends were hidden beneath his closed jacket. He walked up to the maestro, but the latter just went on beckoning with his crooked finger in front of his nose, so Mario had to come even closer, between the legs of the great man, touching the edge of the chair, whereupon Cipolla opened his elbows and grabbed him, setting him a position so we could see his face. He took his time observing him from top to bottom, contemptuous, tyrannical and amused.

'So how can that be, *ragazzo mio*?' he said. 'How is it, young lad, that we're so late getting to know each other? Anyway, believe me, I've known about you for a long while… I've had you in my sights a long while now and reassured myself as to your excellent qualities. How could I ever forget you again? I've had so much to do, you know… Tell me, what's your name? I just need to know your first name.'

'Mario's my name,' answered the young man softly.

'Ah, Mario, very good. Yes, it's a name you hear. A well-known name. A name from antiquity, one of those that keep alive the heroic heritage of the Fatherland. Bravo. *Salve!*' And he stretched his arm and his flat hand out from his shoulder and steeply upwards to make the Roman salute. It wouldn't have been a surprise to learn that he was a bit drunk, but he spoke, now as before, without the slightest slur and fluently, even though by this time something self-satisfied, something of the pasha, a jeering cockiness, had entered into his whole demeanour and was affecting the intonation of his words.

'Right then, young Mario,' he went on, 'it's nice that you've come this evening, and even more to the point that you're wearing such a chic cravat, it suits your face perfectly and will surely get you somewhere with the girls, the charming girls of Torre di Venere…'

From among the standing places, around where Mario himself had been standing, there came the sound of laughter—it came from the *giovanotto* with the military haircut. He was standing there with his jacket over one shoulder and laughing really nastily and mockingly. 'Ha ha!'

Mario just shrugged, I believe. Or he flinched. Perhaps he winced and the movement of his shoulders was a half-hearted attempt to disguise it. In any case he wanted to say that neither his cravat nor the fair sex meant anything to him.

The maestro shot a quick glance down into the audience.

'We needn't bother about him over there,' he said. 'He's jealous, probably because your cravat is so successful with the girls, perhaps also because you and I are having such a nice little chat up here... If he'd like it I could remind him of his stomach cramps. It's no skin off my nose. Come on now, Mario, tell us: tonight you're out for the evening to have fun... and during the day you also work as an assistant in a general store?'

'As a waiter in a café,' the lad corrected him.

'In a café, so that's it!' For once Cipolla hadn't got it quite right. 'You're a *cameriere*, a cupbearer, a Ganymede. I like it. There's another touch of antiquity you bring with you—*salvietta!*[1] And with that, to the delight of the audience, the maestro once again stretched out his arm and gave the salute.

Mario smiled too. 'A while ago,' he added as a kind of corrective, 'I used to work behind the counter in a shop in Portoclemente.' There was something in his remark of a human desire to establish the truth, the relevant details.

'Right, right! In a general store!'

'There were brushes and combs there,' answered Mario evasively.

'Did I not say that you were not always a Ganymede, that you didn't always wait at table? Even when Cipolla gets it wrong, people trust him to come close to getting it right. Tell me, do you trust me?'

Some vague movement.

'Half an answer,' the maestro summed up. 'No doubt it's hard to win your trust. Even for me, I can see that very well, it's not easy. I can discern in your face some trace of resignation, of sadness, *un tratto di malinconia*... Tell me now,' and he grasped Mario's hand as he spoke. He'd spied a touch of melancholy. 'Is something worrying you?'

'*Nossignore!*' came the prompt and definite answer. 'Not on your life! What do you take me for?'

'Something is worrying you,' insisted the entertainer, dismissing the assertion in authoritarian fashion. 'Am I supposed not to notice? Go on you can tell Cipolla! Of course it's girls, a girl is the matter. You have worries of the heart.'

Mario shook his head vigorously. At the same time we heard resounding beside us the brutal laughter of the *giovanotto*. The maestro kept an ear cocked. His eyes were out there somewhere, but he was listening to the laughter and then, as he had done once or twice while talking to Mario, he cracked the riding whip half-backwards in the direction of the little platoon of wrigglers and jigglers, lest any of them lose momentum. While he was doing that, however, he almost lost his partner, for, suddenly coming to himself, the latter turned his back on him and walked towards the steps. He was red around the eyes. Cipolla just managed to hang on to him.

'Stay where you are!' he said. 'Do you mean you want to pack it in, Ganymede, in the best moment, or just before the best moment? Stay here and I can promise you good things. I promise you that I will convince you your fears have no basis. This girl that you know, and whom others know too, this—what was her name? Wait a moment! I can read the name in your eyes, it's on the tip of my tongue, and you, I can see, are on the point of coming out with it...'

'Silvestra!' the *giovanotto*, our young man about town, cried out from below.

The maestro betrayed no change of expression.

'Don't some people just go in for shooting their mouths off?' he asked, without looking out into the audience, rather focusing on his undisturbed conversation with Mario. 'Aren't there always and everywhere cocks who crow too early, who sound off whenever they feel like? What does he think he's doing, stealing the name from our lips, yours and mine? He probably feels, the vain fool, that's he got a special right to own it. Let's leave him be! Silvestra though, your Silvestra, go on, say it, she's some girl, isn't she? A real treasure! One's heart stands still when one sees her walking, breathing, laughing, she's so very charming. And her rounded arms, when she's doing the washing and throwing back her head as she does so and shaking the hair off her face! An angel from paradise!'

Mario shoved his head forwards and stared at him. He seemed to have forgotten where he was and that anyone was watching him. The red flecks in his eyes had grown and looked as if they had been painted on. I've seldom seen that. His thick lips were parted.

'And this angel is giving you trouble,' Cipolla went on, 'or rather you worry about her... There's a difference, my friend, a difference which means there's a great deal in the balance, let me assure you! In love there are misunderstandings—it might be said that misunderstandings are nowhere more at home than here. You will say, what does Cipolla, with his little deformity, know about love? That would be a mistake, in fact he knows a lot about it, he has a very comprehensive and penetrating knowledge of love, and it would be worthwhile for a man in your circumstances to hear him out. But let's leave Cipolla aside, let's leave him out of the game, and think only about Silvestra, your charming Silvestra!

What is it? Did someone say she prefers some crowing cockerel to you, with the result that he can laugh and you must weep? That she prefers someone other than you, who are such a sensitive and kind young lad? That's not only unlikely, it's impossible, we know better, Cipolla and your girl. If I put myself in her place, you see, and have the choice between such an oaf, thick as two planks, as ordinary as a plate of salt fish and *frutti di mare*, and a Mario who is a knight errant of the napkin,[2] who moves in circles, who deals with foreigners and brings them refreshments and who loves me with a warm, true feeling—honestly, my heart has no difficulty in choosing, I know very well to whom I should give it, to whom alone, with a blush, I gave it already long ago. It's time that he sees it and grasps it, my chosen one! It's time that you see me, Mario, and realize… Tell me, who am I?'

It was ghastly, how this impersonator turned himself into the loved one, how he gave a coquettish turn to his lopsided shoulders, made his baggy eyes gaze with longing and revealed his crumbling teeth in a sweet smile. But what had become of Mario during this torrent of false words? It will be hard for me to say it, as it was hard for me to see, but it was a revelation of the deepest passion, the public expression of a desperate and delusional bliss. He held his hands pressed together in front of his lips, his shoulders rose and fell in violent sobs. Clearly he couldn't believe his eyes and ears for the happiness he felt and forgot only one thing therein, that he really couldn't trust them. 'Silvestra!' he whispered, overcome, from somewhere deep in his heart.

'Kiss me!' said the hunchback. 'Believe me, you are allowed to kiss me! I love you. Kiss me here,' and he pointed with the tip of his index finger, forcing his hand, arm and little finger out of the way, to his cheek, close to his lips. And Mario bent over and kissed him.

It was so quiet in the auditorium you could hear a pin drop. The moment was grotesque, outrageous, and people wondered what would come next—that moment of Mario's bliss. In that terrible space of time, in which all the possibilities of happiness and illusion overwhelmed his emotions, what one could hear, although not immediately, but straight after the distressing and scurrilous contact Mario's lips made with that repugnant flesh that committed itself to be the object of his tenderness, was the laughter of the *giovanotto* to our left. It was the only response to be heard, and it was brutal and full of schadenfreude but also, unless I was very much mistaken, not without an undertone of pity for a man so misled in his dreams, not entirely devoid of an inclination to agree with whoever in the audience had previously cried out '*poveretto!*', which the magician had declared to be directed at the wrong person and had claimed for himself.

Before the laughter had died away, however, the man who had been so affectionately kissed on his cheek, as it were at the summit of his being, reached below into the lower depths, beside the leg of his chair, and cracked his whip, and Mario, as he woke up, started and stepped backwards. He stood and stared, his body bent over forwards, pressed his hands one over the other against his misused lips, rapped his knuckles several times against the side of his head, and then, as the audience applauded and Cipolla, with his hands folded in his lap, chuckled—you could just see his shoulders rocking—the young man turned abruptly and rushed down the steps. Once below, in continuous motion, he hurled himself about, his legs going everywhere, then he lifted up his arm and the dull thud of two shots rang out, transfusing the applause and the laughter.

Everything fell silent. Even the jumping jacks came to a halt and looked on dismayed. Cipolla had all of a sudden leapt up from his chair. He stood there with his arms outstretched either side of him, as if keeping people at bay, as if he wanted to say: 'Stop! Be quiet! Everyone get away from me! What's going on?' But in the next moment he slumped back into his chair with his head flopped on to his chest and almost immediately fell sideways from it, on to the floor, where he remained lying, motionless, a great messy bundle of clothes and bones all askew.

The uproar was never-ending. Ladies who were sobbing and shaking hid their faces in the chests of their companions. Someone rang for a doctor, and for the police. People stormed up on to the stage. In all the confusion they hurled themselves at Mario to disarm him. They relieved him of the tiny, dull, metal mechanism hardly worthy of being called a pistol and that was hanging in his hand, he whose barely existent career fate had dragged in such an unforeseen and alien direction.

We took the children—at last, you may say—and made our way, past the pair of *carabinieri* who had just entered, to the exit. 'Was that actually the end?' they wanted to know, to be sure. 'Yes, that was the end,' we confirmed. A shocking end. A fateful end, and no mistake. But also, at the same time, a liberating end—I couldn't help then, as now, feeling that way.

(1930)

Afterword

Thomas Mann said all his works were part of a single great confession. Those words alluded to Germany's greatest literary figure, Johann Wolfgang von Goethe, and announced Mann's towering ambition to be a writer who would also make fictional use of his own life. Goethe, born in 1749, had written his landmark *The Sorrows of Young Werther* (1774) aged twenty-five. Mann, born in 1875, wrote *Tonio Kröger* (1903) when he was twenty-eight. In turn that story contained, in embryo, almost all the personal and artistic themes he would return to throughout his career.

Mann had become famous overnight with his massive and hugely engaging first novel *Buddenbrooks* (1901). *Tonio Kröger* was the miniature counterpart to that family saga. Both the novel and the story were set in the north German city of Lübeck, the old Hanseatic port on the Baltic Sea where Mann grew up as the second son of a wealthy patrician family. He avowed he had a happy childhood and his pride in his family's high social and moral standing marks all the stories in this collection. A writer who became the greatest literary witness of Germany's fate under Hitler, Mann lived through profound changes in his country from the start of the First World War. He was a democrat, but he remained nostalgic for the comfortable, opulent, richly ordered upper-middle-class life he first knew. That bourgeois or middle-class ideal also recurs, often nostalgically, in these stories spanning almost thirty years.

Mann was fifteen when his father died suddenly. The highly respected grain business was liquidated and the house sold. In 1891 his mother, of Portuguese origin, moved the family to Munich, as far south in Germany as it was possible to get, away from the chilly, damp Baltic north. Mann continued his education but he never got on well with educational institutions and for a few years in Munich worked in a fire insurance company before becoming a literary journalist. After he published his first story in 1898 his extraordinary artistic success began.

In *Tonio Kröger* the eponymous hero is equally split between the orderly, conventional and delightful routines he knew as a boy and the exotic adventure of a life in art. He too has moved to Munich, but finds that literary achievement and a high reputation have not made him happy. He has a profound distrust of the art he practises. All this he confesses to his Russian friend, the artist Lisaveta Ivanovna, whose gentle puncturing of his self-importance sets the ironic tone for the narrative that ensues. Their friendship allows Tonio to talk about what art means to him and to explore the third, overarching theme of Mann's career, alongside the passing of the bourgeoisie and the coming of Hitler, namely what it means to be a *German* writer.

Art for Mann is the literary art above all. But he distinguished sharply between the life of the *Literat*, the professional wordsmith, and the *Dichter*, the upholder of a great German philosophical and cultural tradition, whose devout task, in Mann's view, was to give classical Form to inchoate events and emotions. In the key confession to Lisaveta Ivanovna, I've capitalized the terms Art and Life. Tonio Kröger is the most philosophical of the three stories, and it is the mismatch between the moral value of Art—its pretensions—and Life—its naivety—that is its true subject.

Like many outsiders, Tonio aged fourteen loves those almost aggressively normal characters around him who tend not even to notice his love. Hans Hansen and Ingeborg Holm are from their early years physically attractive, socially successful, 'normal' human beings whereas Tonio is awkward and odd. The comedy and the tragedy of his situation is that these 'normal' people are the ones he loves and wants to be among; he despises other outsiders. Ironically, it seems to him that all his writerly striving is just an attempt to have himself accepted in 'ordinary' society.

It is how he navigates his own social conservatism, despite his extraordinary intellectual and artistic sophistication, that is Mann's fundamental story, and that perhaps is the fourth theme here, his deep desire to affirm 'normality'. Whether the cause of unhappiness is misplaced sexual longing, or social or political disturbance, or merely a persistent sense of being an outsider, he seeks ways in which misery can be left behind and evil set at bay.

In *Tonio Kröger* the hero moves from being a teenage misfit to being an anti-bourgeois aesthetic radical before finally returning to his roots. He comes home, albeit as a stranger, but content to be an adoring observer. The stories are amused and ironic, as they drive towards their celebrations of 'normal' feeling. Sometimes it has seemed to critics almost as if they are written for two distinct audiences—a more naïve readership on the one hand, wanting to watch moments of that recognizable ordinariness unfold, and an undeceived, intellectually more knowing audience demanding acknowledgement of more awkward truths. Yet Mann's achievement, as a master storyteller and a highly idiosyncratic thinker, was precisely to appeal to both. He blended naturalism and irony, simple human affection and remarkable intellectual adventurousness in a unique contribution to literary modernism.

His characteristically elaborate descriptions of people and places are devoted to the rituals of middle-class life, and especially in *Tonio Kröger* to the weather he loved in that maritime northern clime. He uses words like brushstrokes, constantly adding to the picture, to deepen and add texture to his vision. Food, clothes and bodily and facial characteristics are almost photographically reproduced. Another stylistic trait is how he attaches to particular characters and their situations a recurrent verbal theme or *leitmotif*. This is then repeated every time they enter the scene. (Mann borrowed the idea from Wagnerian opera.) Hans Hansen, Ingeborg Holm and also the two Kröger parents live in our minds by way of these short identifying phrases. Mann brings to the human situation both amusement and tenderness, as well as, he often adds, just a little bit of contempt for how fixed in our ways we all are; how our appearance labels us.

Mann's homosexuality, about which the world learnt so much from the diaries published after his death in 1955, is not an explicit theme in *Tonio Kröger*, though for today's reader it suggests another obvious reason for his feeling outside society and needing to find a form in which to confess that dilemma. As he finished and published this story, Mann decided to give himself a 'constitution'—to make the social structure of his life more secure—and, rather than take the bohemian path, to anchor himself in upper-middle-class life by way of marriage. He wanted a loving family, social rank and acceptance. And so in 1905 he married Katia Pringsheim, the much-sought-after daughter of a far wealthier, far grander family than his own. They had six children, and their bond remained solid throughout a challenging life.

How much he adored the would-be conventional family life they made together became the subject of the second story here, *Disorder and Early Sorrow*. Published in 1925, this tale was another affirmation of social conservatism in trying personal circumstances which included sexual and political confusion. In this story the old upper-middle-class life has been undone by Germany's defeat in the First World War, by the passing of the Kaiser and his empire, and by rampant economic inflation. The quirks of human sexuality emerge as part of a more general social revolution that is both funny and for the older generation unnerving.

Disorder and Early Sorrow is another beguiling, mesmerizing work, another tapestry of rich social description interlaced with deeper, darker thoughts about sexuality, history and from a writer's point of view what one might call the uses of melancholy. This is expressed by its leading character, Professor Cornelius. 'Disorder' is not only the state of the household as it prepares for a party, nor even the troubled state of Weimar Germany, which has swept aside many of the traditions and rules that governed Mann's earlier life. It is also Abel Cornelius's love for his five-year-old daughter Lorchen which seems even to himself as at once the greatest thing in the world and in its intensity rather suspect. A sudden outburst of erotic passion on Lorchen's own part challenges—as Sigmund Freud did at the time—not only long-held beliefs in childhood innocence but makes her own father jealous. Abel Cornelius is also distinctly interested in the manly charms of his manservant, who just happens to resemble his own teenage son Bert.

In a less inhibited age, highly characteristic of the Weimar Republic that constituted the German state between the wars, these forbidden loves ever more boldly spoke their name. Mann relished them, but feared the threat to the family life they seemed to present. If we compare this story with *Death in Venice* (1912), however, we can see that whereas Mann 'confessed' his homosexuality tragically and front-of-stage in that earlier story, thirteen years later he finds his sexual ambivalence mostly melancholy and faintly comic.

Disorder and Early Sorrow explores all the intricacies and varieties of human physical attachment, across the conventional boundaries of age and gender, and asks us to smile at them and tolerate them. Through Tonio Kröger, Mann began by saying that his whole art was about combining the comedy and the tragedy, or simply the misery of so many human lives. But clearly *Disorder* took his art into a new dimension when it drew its devastating analogy between the personal and the political. If the love we depend upon to anchor our lives has no more stability and coherence than, say, German politics in a time of turmoil, what can we hope for in our deepest humanity? If such instability lurks behind ordinary Life, perhaps we do best to pretend we haven't noticed. We may prefer to follow Professor Cornelius's example and look upon the beauty of a sleeping child with the cry, 'Thank heaven for that!' Following just a year after his intellectually complex novel *The Magic Mountain* (1924), *Disorder and Early Sorrow* was, again, a great achievement in miniature of a fifty-year-old writer at the peak of his powers.

Reading—and indeed relishing—the subtext of this rich story, we might want to pay particular attention to the servant Xaver Kleinsgütl, who with his exotic first name and German surname (just like Tonio Kröger in the earlier story) is an out and out social disrupter and yet with a heart of gold. A chippy working-class lad, he is both an insolent onlooker and a loyal servant who saves the five-year-old Lorchen in her hour of distress. His ironic treatment may owe something to the eponymous servant in Mozart's *The Marriage of Figaro*, another classic tale blending revolutionary politics, new social equality and sexual licence.

The theme of innocence was so important to Mann. What can it mean for us, given what we know about human nature? Mann was interested in all the delicate currents of attraction and repulsion that bind us together but are mostly neither spoken nor acted upon. Can that restraint also not be a kind of decency, he asked, even if murkier desires run just beneath the surface? In *Death in Venice* Gustav von Aschenbach agonized over whether his passion for a beautiful fourteen-year-old boy must lead inevitably to what is in our time criminal lust. Aschenbach tried to repress the physical longing, even as it overwhelmed him. *Disorder and Early Sorrow* says that even if it's true that such suspect feelings exist, some so dark as to threaten to destroy us, Life itself is about having desires and Life must go on. Society tells us that some desires are shameful and even criminal, but when we reflect in the privacy of our own minds on what we feel, melancholy, not shame, might be the better response. Melancholy is a civilizing emotion, it is on the side of Life, and even in our darker moments, in conjunction with restraint, it can save us.

Mario and the Magician, published in 1930, juxtaposed the innocence that children represent with the political scurrilousness that was asserting itself in Fascist Italy when Mann and his family holidayed there four years earlier. Where he had previously been concerned with social normality versus sexual ambivalence, here he explored the blurred line dividing entertainment from political manipulation. Starting perhaps from the fact that his family affectionately called him 'The Magician', he began to imagine the *Zauberkünstler* Cipolla, a wandering player who turns up to entertain the people and tourists of the imagined resort of Torre di Venere ('Tower of Venus'). *Mario* is a story about irrationality, persuasion and the lurking evil in human nature. But it is also about another of Mann's underlying concerns, namely, since we are all are in some sense manipulators, what divides the serious, would-be moral writer-artist from his less scrupulous counterparts in politics and daily life.

The Mann family holidayed on the Tyrrhenian Sea, not far from Portovenere, and much of the story derived from their actual experience, as the author confirmed in a letter.[1] His first impulse was to relegate the 'elements of critical idealism and political morality' in the story to a secondary role. But there would be no story worth reading today without the author's sense of the moral and political drama at stake. That drama was about how easily, in an Italy stirred with populist and nationalist sentiment, locals and holidaymakers alike could fall for a confidence trickster and accept his degrading and humiliating treatment of his willing victims. Even the narrator and his wife cannot tear themselves away from the mesmerizing spectacle and they risk the innocence of their children by staying.

A contemporary reader may have some difficulty grasping all the predetermined ways in which the crippled Cipolla is depicted as evil, for they concern his ugly, deformed body, his ingratiating manner with others, and his underlying quasi-Nietzschean desire to be avenged on ordinary life, in which he occupies such an inferior position. The reader may feel that this aspect of the story is in poor taste. Indeed it is by present-day standards, but it belongs, along with many comments in all the stories on different national and ethnic characteristics, and an exaggerated attention to physiognomy, and a willingness to draw moral inferences from physical appearances, to a climate of European thought that dominated cultural attitudes from the 1890s to the Second World War. Popularizations of both Nietzsche and Darwin went into its making, leading to the notion of degeneracy taken up by the Nazis to justify their murderous racism. To clarify Mann's actual feelings, we should remember that one of the bad selves he shed in his fiction, Aschenbach in *Death in Venice*, began as the embodiment of enlightened culture and moral decency and fell into *Entartung*—degeneracy through giving in to his fatal homoerotic desires. The parallel in *Mario* is the risk run by ordinary decent people, like the narrator and his family, when they let themselves be misled by dubious trickery into condoning manipulation and cruelty. It is painful to us today to see Mann identify homoeroticism with decadence and even further with political decadence. But these are stories about Mann's personal struggle to be a good family man upholding the old bourgeois order in society. For that his protagonists have to accept the need to choose the right path, according to the decency of the times, even if in their heart of hearts their feelings are more wayward; or, in *Mario*, even if they are tempted to toy with evil out of fascination. The name Cipolla—meaning onion in Italian—is of course already ironic and invites the reader to establish a sound moral distance from the decadent *artiste* who is also a Fascist sympathizer. But still the unnamed narrator falls under his sway and cannot properly account for why, as a cultured, educated man, he does not take his children away; why he stays in that corrupt 'Venusian' atmosphere in the first place.

Mann said a political lesson had not been his intention in the story, but one feels that was to protect its integrity as art, as Mann saw it. It is also the case than in *Mario* he was not only thinking about Fascist Italy but also about increasing political violence in Germany that was sweeping the crowds along. In a diary entry in 1934 he would comment that the present extreme times elevated 'a purely natural, evil notion' of politics over the normal humane elements that belonged to it. Politics had become 'the philosophy of predators' because

> people are infected and seduced; because there is a general weakness in human beings that makes them all too easily forget the cultural-intellectual side of their nature and abandon themselves

to the purely natural... and so the whole continent runs the danger of falling into bloody violence and barbarity and of going to ruin. And the irony of the story would be, that the country that brought about this end would be the one that became the most reflective and spiritual of peoples out of its original noble inability to deal with the things of the external and the real world.[2]

The topic is too vast to explore here, but what he had in mind was yet another kind of innocence gone astray. He was thinking of nineteenth-century Germany's exalted faith in a humanism sustained by Art and the Artist; thinking of the German cultural tradition in which he himself was educated; and the twentieth-century catastrophe Germany became. He felt his own partial involvement in that collective delusion, one might say, when he wrote *Mario and the Magician*, and thus the story was also in some sense a prelude to his novel *Doktor Faustus* (1947).

It's this interweaving of his deepest worries about himself, about the potentially fraudulent nature of art, and the fate of European society around him that makes Thomas Mann a great writer. He finds in exposing political errancy a superb use for the deep melancholy his outsider status has inspired in himself since late childhood. One has to stand back. One should not become passionately, violently, deludedly engaged on one side or another, only try to understand human complexity. Early in Mann's life his character Lisaveta Ivanovna—the Russian, the artist but with a non-German point of view—saw Tonio Kröger as a good bourgeois gone wrong: *ein verirrter Bürger*. Fifty years later, this was Mann's verdict on his own country: that a good Germany had gone astray. His judgement should surely have been more severe; but it remained the country that he loved and which he tried to explain to the world.

In my view, *Mario* is a magnificent work of literature that does not quite hang together. The incidents in the first hotel and on the beach, with the coarse and brutal lower-class boy Fuggièro, and the outrage over the little German girl running naked while washing her swimming costume, link together a mindless national pride in the mass of the people and a prudish, narrow-minded, insular moralizing of what at the time would have been called the petty bourgeoisie. It was on their support, history would show, that both the Mussolini and Hitler regimes could call. The connection between this moral primitivism, dressed up as small-town propriety, and including a dislike of foreigners, and the designs of a Cipolla on the whole human race can be made; but it takes work on the part of the reader to see that in all these cases, for Mann, an enlightened, middle-class, liberal culture which respects the dignity of individuals is at risk. On the other hand, once that connection is accepted, the story flows inexorably.

Two other features of it stand out. One is the undertow of Greek myth, with its metamorphoses often carried out by the gods for dubious erotic purposes and with tragic human results. The second is the tribute Mann cannot help paying to great works of German literature, in this case to Heinrich von Kleist's famous essay on 'The Puppet Theatre', a classic exploration of what happens when human beings are deprived of the power to exercise their own will.

All three stories here were part of Mann's quest, as a writer, to purge himself of moral ambivalence and affirm the value of normal, ordinary Life unambiguously. All three testify to his love of language and languages. My aim as a translator, in recasting them into English, has been to minimize the obstacles that arise because of Mann's formidable style and intellect. The way the German language so beautifully obeys his purposes is not always to be felt in equivalent English prose. It has seemed important to capture every nuance of the original, which has sometimes meant expanding a single German word into an English phrase or entire clause. Typical Mann sentences are often long and complex, but they never lose their balance, and it's important that the English equivalents should also not lurch and stagger. Mann's sentences contain great chains of adjectives and adverbs modifying those adjectives, conveying all the shimmering and foaming, the creaking, raging and groaning, over the sea and in the wind, and the human merriment, on the windswept Baltic shore, somewhat in contrast to a sultry, stifling Italian seaside resort where the burning sun behind a grey sky spreads a terrible lassitude; all the eyebrow-raising and puzzling and blushing, all the intent gazes that go in the wrong direction, all the intricate outfits that people wear to reflect their character, their sexuality and their social class, and the kind of food they enjoyed once ago in a high-class German salon. Some of these descriptions are offered almost as lists, without verbs to animate them. Mann's punctuation, a mass of dashes and semi-colons, erratic as it is, keeps the artistic process just under control. His ellipses carry heavy hints. Sometimes his descriptions give way to streams of consciousness. The writing is confident and expansive, and I've tried to stay in step.

LESLEY CHAMBERLAIN

LONDON, SEPTEMBER 2024

Notes

1   A nihilist in nineteenth-century Russia was a terrorist committed to acts of violence against the state.
2   A reference to Niccolò Machiavelli (1469–1527), with whom Mann associated an amoral devotion to worldly success.

DISORDER AND EARLY SORROW

1   An originally Egyptian game whereby two players sit on the floor, legs and hands outstretched, the feet touching, the hands linked together, and the third player has to jump over the obstacle. They start at floor level and gradually raise and widen the hurdle. It was popular in Germany at the turn of the twentieth century.
2   Italian salad – this was probably what in other countries was popularly known, since the mid-nineteenth-century, as 'Russian salad'. It would have been made with cooked vegetables including potatoes and carrots, chopped ham, pickles and mayonnaise, although the inventive cook could use any meat that came to hand. For Mann to specify the recipe is once more to indicate the straitened circumstances, already announced in the first paragraph, of this otherwise wealthy upper-middle-class German family after Germany's defeat in the First World War.
3   The years of rampant inflation in Weimar Germany began in 1921 and peaked in 1923 when paper money became almost worthless. According to the Treaty of Versailles (1919), Germany's settlement with the victors in the 1914–18 conflict entailed paying exorbitant reparations. The crisis was fuelled by government borrowing to

finance those debts and hit middle-class families with savings particularly hard.

4 Another indication of Germany's economic difficulties at the time of this story.

5 Hans von Marées (1837–87), German painter.

6 The familiar form of 'you' in German, at the time only used between family members and close friends and to children.

7 The reference here may be, indirectly, to Sigmund Freud's theory of the *Fehlleistung*, the psychological slip, whereby a person means to say one thing and ends up saying another which is actually a closer reflection of what they truly desired, but were repressing for the sake of social propriety. Possibly here the homosexual actor who says literally that he is 'most bound' to his host recognizes the repressed homosexuality of Doctor Cornelius that would 'bind them together'. Mann uses the word '*Entgleisung*', which means a lapse into tactless, unseemly or inappropriate behaviour.

8 'Sire, my liege, give me your daughter.'

9 Matthew 7:16.

10 *The Prince of Pappenheim* (*Der Fürst von Pappenheim*, 1922) was a highly successful three-act operetta by Hugo Kirsch. In 1927 a German silent comedy film about an ambitious young man in the new post-war Germany, set to become famous in the history of cinema, was based upon it.

11 The reference is to a famous quartet of qualities advocated for young people (and inscribed on the outside wall of his house) by the founder of the German gymnastics movement, '*Turnvater*' Friedrich Ludwig Jahn, in 1816. Mann, who evidently viewed the idea of '*frisch-fromm-fröhliche Entschlossenheit*' with irony and as culturally philistine, omitted the fourth quality, 'free'. Nazi Germany would appropriate Jahn's slogan to encourage the Hitler Youth Movement.

12 The reference is to Goethe's poem of 1795.

13 A repetition of the line from *The Prince of Pappenheim* already quoted by Cornelius's daughter Ingrid.

MARIO AND THE MAGICIAN: A TRAGIC HOLIDAY MEMORY

1   Mann makes a pun by combining the Italian for napkin, or the tea towel a waiter might carry over his forearm, *salvietta*, with the greeting '*salve!*' which was associated with the Roman salute.

2   These extravagant neologisms, also strange to German readers, are Mann's own and are translated literally. The ordinariness of those fish dishes—at least in Torre di Venere—stands for the undistinguished person of Mario's rival in love, whereas he himself is *der Ritter der Serviette*.

AFTERWORD

1   To Otto Hoerth, 12 June 1930, in *The Letters of Thomas Mann 1889–1955*, selected and translated by Richard and Clara Winston (Harmondsworth: Penguin, 1975), pp. 153–5.

2   Thomas Mann 'Leiden an Deutschland'('Sorrow over Germany'), *Gesammelte Werke* (1955), vol. 12, p. 175.